'Lost & Found'

3.5 Silk & Steel

Ariana Nash

Dark Fantasy Author

Subscribe to Ariana's mailing list here.

FOREWORD

After wrapping up the Silk & Steel trilogy, I thought I was done with this world. But even as I typed The End after Blood & Ice, and Lysander and Eroan had gone off on some adventure, one little thing niggled the back of my mind: Trey.

From the short story prequel, Sealed with a Kiss, fans fell in love with the kind-hearted messenger. He then went on to feature in the main series, proving himself to be a truly good character and friend when needed the most. He stood by Eroan, even when he didn't agree with some of his choices, and he fought for what's right, like all good Assassins of the Order.

We don't know exactly what happened between Trey and Nye, but we can guess. And after everyone else got their happy ending, Trey's ending just didn't sit right with me. He needed closure, and so did we.

That's where Lost & Found comes in. Trey's story. It takes place AFTER the trilogy and contains spoilers for the Silk & Steel series, so be sure to read the Silk & Steel trilogy first.

The Silk & Steel world has a special place in my heart. The characters touched me like none other in my entire writing career. I'm terribly sad to see it over, and yet thrilled that these books are in the hands of thousands of readers world-wide, who truly love these dragons and elves as much as I do.

Words are not enough, but they'll have to do: Thank you for everything, Dear Reader.

Now, enjoy Trey's story...

~

Trey had always been a wanderer. "Little Restless Feet," his mother had called him as an elfling. She'd laugh, ruffle his hair, and tell him he'd wander right off the edge of Alumn's world.

He'd wandered far one day, trying to find this elusive edge of the world, thinking he might find Alumn. He'd ask the goddess to keep his ma and pa safe from dragons. But he'd gotten lost, gotten turned around in the endless forest. The trees had grown bigger and tracks moved, or so it seemed. Then he'd spotted the village lantern's glowing and stumbled home, not knowing a monster stalked him.

What happened after was the same story told up and down the land, and the reason why most elves were orphans.

Now, Trey didn't get lost.

He wasn't *supposed* to get lost. But the seasons had waxed and waned since he'd last trekked this way. Saplings had sprung up, old oaks cut down. He was sure this path led across the moor to the elven capital of Ashford, and yet... not. He checked the early evening skies, looking for the reassuring twinkle of the North Star but found only heavy cloud cover.

Cold air nipped at his face, night approaching. If he didn't reach familiar ground soon, he'd have to make camp without shelter. He walked on, carving through low brush, following what could have been an old elf track or an animal track. If it were an elf track, the scrub had grown over, meaning it was little-used. Another sign he was on the wrong path.

He adjusted the blade on its belt hook and the backpack. The shortsword bumped reassuringly against his thigh. Smaller than most Order dragonblades, Eroan Ilanea had crafted it personally, knowing Trey would prefer the weapon be light and fast. Eroan had given him the sword as a parting gift, as though he'd known for weeks that Trey had been gathering the courage to ask to return to his messenger ways.

Technically, Trey was still an Assassin of the Order, even if the Order had mostly dissolved. With the dragons now tamed, the Order assassins had found themselves out of work. Some had fallen into new lives, pairing up, creating families, staking out claims and tending the land. Eroan had fallen into adventures in far off lands, accompanied by his dragon, Lysander. And Trey had fallen back into wandering. He'd seen enough bloodshed to last a lifetime. The Order way hadn't really been his way.

He huffed a sigh and stopped to eye his surroundings. Mounds of thistle and brambles knotted alongside the path, making camping impossible. The spindly trees were too small to support a hammock. His best bet was to hike higher onto the moor where the grass fell away, leaving rocky outcrops. He squinted at the exposed rocks. He could make a fire there, deterring hungry wolves. There were no dragons around to be lured by firelight, and even if there were, they shied away from elves.

He veered off the path and used his dragonblade to cut

through the brush. Trekking higher until the brambles released him onto open moorland. Crickets chirped and a swift breeze hissed across the land. A familiar, contented smile lifted his lips. He'd forgotten how much he'd missed this. He enjoyed the company of others, but nothing settled the soul like miles and miles of unbroken landscape.

He dumped his bag beside a tumble of huge boulders, put there by ancient glaciers, and set to work making a fire. The flame from his flint and steel caught a bunch of kindling quickly and soon grew into leaping flames. He cleared a space, rolled out a bed mat, rummaged around in the back for the berries he'd found during the day, and settled in the shadow of the boulders for the night.

He'd made a life out of traveling from settlement to settlement, delivering messages and gifts from elf to elf. He knew the rise and fall of the land like the back of his hand, could trek for miles blindfolded. At least, he had been able to. Until the Order put a blade in his hand, telling him to fight dragons. He'd always been a lover, not a fighter. A messenger of words and gifts, not death. His backpack was laden with wax-sealed notes and little, wrapped gifts for loved ones in faraway lands.

Belly full, body warm, he dozed, thinking of the smiles and joy his arrival in Ashford would spark.

An out of place noise wrenched his sleep-addled mind awake. The fire had burned down to glowing embers, barely bright enough to hold back the thick dark. Dreams woke him sometimes, bad ones, sharp and loud with screams and the smell of burning bodies. But he hadn't been dreaming of the dark times. Something *had* woken him. Wolves?

He reached for his blade, propped against the rock beside him.

"Looking for this?"

The cool edge of a blade bit at his neck, freezing Trey

still. A ragged-looking elf crouched in front of him. His patched leathers and knotted hair spoke of a life on the road. Tribal tattoos like Trey's snaked up the left side of his face.

"Nice blade." The male cocked his head. "You of the Order, eh?"

Trey swallowed.

Another figure moved in the dark into the warm campfire glow. Taller and slimmer than Ragged, with long golden hair. He upended Trey's backpack and rained the contents across the ground. Gifts and letters, notes that families would have been waiting months for. Tokens of love and friendship. Tossed about as though worthless. Goldie crouched and rummaged through the little parcels. He snatched up one, tore the wrapping off, frowned at the carving of a dragon, and tossed it into the dark.

Trey's cheek twitched. "Keep your hands off those."

Ragged's wide grin was the brightest thing about him. The rest of his clothes, all shades of black, suggested he knew exactly how to blend into the darkness, and he'd done it before.

Bandits. Trey had heard rumor of bands of thieves operating near Ashford, but he'd dismissed it as gossip. No elf would attack another between settlements, that wasn't their way. But clearly, dragons weren't the only ones who had changed since the war.

"Just a bunch of trinkets," Goldie said with a huff, still ripping open letters and parcels, looking for something of value. The letters were priceless, just not to these thieves.

"Keep searching. He'll have something of value. They always do."

Trey held Ragged's glare. The male wasn't afraid. Delight danced in his eyes and on his lips.

"Killed any dragons, eh, Order boy? This little blade hardly looks big enough."

Trey's mouth ticked. "It's not about size—"

"Ha, think you're clever, do you?" Ragged straightened and stepped back, sneering down at Trey. He raked his assessing glare from head to toe. "Did they kick you out the Order? Not good enough, eh?"

"Got something!" Goldie crowed. He turned a chunk of amethyst over in his hand and tossed it to Ragged.

Ragged reached up to catch the stone. Trey lunged, dropping his shoulder. He struck Ragged's thighs, toppling him into the dirt. The sword skipped from Ragged's hand. Goldie raced to grab it. Trey scrabbled for it too. Hands grabbed his ankle and yanked. He kicked out, striking hardness. Ragged grunted. The grip on Trey's ankle loosened and Trey bolted.

Goldie snatched up the blade, inches from Trey's fingers. He backed up and twirled the sword theatrically in his hand, grinning like a bastard.

Trey was on his feet now, Goldie in front of him and Ragged rubbing his jaw beyond. The remnants of the torn packages lay in the dirt all around. Never, in all his years, had Trey ever failed to make a delivery. These two assholes weren't going to stop him from making this one either. He darted his gaze from front to behind, switching from Goldie to Ragged.

Trey had fought dragons. He'd fought in the Ashford battle when the air had been so thick with blood he'd felt as though he was drowning in it. These two fools were nothing.

Ragged lunged from behind. He flung his arms around Trey's middle, clamping Trey in his embrace. Trey swung his head back, impacting hard with some part that cracked and buckled. Ragged swore. Trey doubled over, throwing his weight under him and Ragged forward, over his back, slamming the male into the dirt.

Goldie stabbed the sword forward, but his aim was loose and his balance all wrong. Trey dodged the attack, grabbed

Goldie's wrist and twisted, wrenching a high-pitched scream from the male. Goldie dropped to his knees. Trey leaned into the awkward angle, putting pressure on Goldie's fragile wrist, pushing him down into the dirt. Maybe he'd break every bone in his wrist as punishment for ripping open those letters—

A punch landed low on Trey's back, briefly stealing his air and blurring his vision. Ragged had recovered.

Goldie jabbed an elbow into the back of Trey's knee, knocking him to the ground, and now they were both in the dirt, wrestling for the sword. Trey clawed and scrabbled for the blade in Goldie's hand, but the bastard managed to hold it high and slammed his forehead into Trey's.

"Get him!" Ragged screeched.

But then Ragged suddenly thumped to his knees, face frozen in shock. The huge arrow sticking from his chest likely had something to do with that.

Trey froze. Goldie saw his companion and screamed.

Ragged looked down at the arrow with its silver shaft and red fletchings, frowned, and toppled facedown in the dirt.

An Ashford sentinel emerged from the dark like Alumn had shaped flame into male form and set it free upon the land. He held a longbow aloft, arrow nocked and string pulled back. Red hair, done up in tight braids, turquoise eyes, and a killer's snarl. Firelight danced over Ashford's silver sigil of a tree stitched to his coat.

Humans believed in avenging angels. Terrifying figures of power and righteous judgment. Trey did not, until now.

Goldie scrabbled to his feet, holding Trey's sword out like a talisman against evil spirits.

"Drop the blade," the Ashford sentinel ordered, voice hard but empty.

Goldie flung the blade down and lifted both hands. "Shit—"

The sentinel's arrow flew, punched Goldie in the chest

6

and flung him backward off his feet. He sprawled in the dirt and lay gasping, until falling still.

The bandit had surrendered, tossed down his weapon, and the sentinel had killed him anyway.

The quiet was back. Trey swallowed. He was still on his knees, only now he was flanked by two dead bodies and a sentinel. He looked up, recognition punching home. The pinned and restrained red hair, the harsh cheekbones and thin lips. Trey knew him. Anyone who had fought for Ashford knew Sentinel Venali. Word was he'd single-handedly killed fifty dragons with his red-feathered arrows. Some of those rumors put the number closer to a hundred. The number climbed with every village Trey visited. Outside of Eroan, Venali had the next most bloodthirsty reputation.

"You didn't have to kill them," Trey heard himself say.

Venali narrowed his eyes. "They would have killed you."

"You don't know that—"

"I do. Actually." He slung the bow over his shoulder and approached Ragged's cooling body. Using his boot, he rolled the bandit onto his back, grasped the arrow, and yanked it free with as much thought as pulling a knife through a piece of meat.

Trey climbed to his feet as Venali retrieved his second arrow from Goldie, only this time, he needed to put some weight behind the tug. He planted a boot on Goldie's chest and heaved. Now that he had his arrows back, a tiny hint of a smile lifted the corners of his lips. He plucked a cloth from his frock coat pocket and wiped the arrows clean before sliding them back into the quiver on his back. Then he turned and headed back into the dark.

"Wait."

Venali turned, eyebrow raised.

"You can't just leave them here like this...?"

Contempt further narrowed Venali's eyes. Maybe he was

used to others quaking before him, but Trey had fought in the same battle, had seen the same horrors, and he knew damn well Venali had the same nightmares. Witnessing monstrous things didn't have to turn people into monsters too.

"It's all they deserve," Venali rumbled.

Was he really this callous? "They need to be buried and guided to Alumn's garden."

Venali started forward, coming straight for Trey as though he'd found his new prey and would stalk it to its death. He stopped inches from Trey, brilliant turquoise eyes searching Trey's.

Trey had been wrong, Alumn hadn't crafted him from fire, she'd chipped him out of pure, hard ice. His eyes weren't warm but cold and shallow. Maybe he had killed a hundred dragons. He certainly looked like he could.

As he looked through Trey, he must have found something, because his glare softened by the smallest margin. It was still full of ice, but some of it had melted. "I've been tracking those two for weeks. Before you, they'd killed five. A young couple for their fine clothes and a pride of three for no other reason than because they could. They left their victims' bodies to rot on the roads into Ashford. If you want to bury them, go ahead. I'm not wasting another second of my life on creatures like them."

He turned in a swirl of red coat and was gone in a few strides, leaving Trey staring into the dark.

ASHFORD GLEAMED IN THE SUNLIGHT. In the past, the largest elven settlement had been buried beneath a thousand years of rubble, like most old human settlements, but the Ashford council had kept it buried and secret for safety. Excavations to clear the enormous site had begun shortly after the end of the war. Now, with the earth moved aside, the buildings appeared to be sprouting out of the ground and toward the light. Vast gardens had sprung up on the approach. Elves from all over the land sauntered through rose-walks and meandered through the lawns. The contrast with how Trey had last seen the place, surrounded by pyres and choked by smoke, gave him pause. The war and its deaths hadn't been for nothing. The world really was changing.

He drifted down the main concourse and headed inside by way of a gloriously chiseled stone archway. Ashford's interior shone, too, all patched up, rebuilt, and freshly painted. The huge, ancient tree continued to stand proud in the central atrium. Half its branches were missing from where a dragon had fallen through the glass ceiling and stripped it bare, but the rest was in full summer leaf. It made a fitting monument for an elven society rising out of the ashes.

Trey made his presence known at the arrivals area and handed over the backpack at a very official-looking desk carved from oak. After burying the two bandits, he'd salvaged every single message, gift, and note and carefully rewrapped them. Everyone would get their messages, and in a few days, he'd set off again with a new batch of deliveries.

"Welcome, messenger!" The young male at the desk beamed. "My name is Conor, and I'm delighted to act as your assistant during your stay. If you have any questions or concerns, come straight to me." He wore his hair short, as seemed to be the fashion of late. The wavy chestnut locks licked at his cheeks and jaw, emphasizing a warm face. One made for smiling.

"Thank you, and call me Trey, please." Trey handed over his bag, wincing a little at its filthy, frayed edges. "I had some issues."

Conor took the bag and checked over the contents, then regarded Trey's equally disheveled clothes. His gaze lingered longer than was necessary. "Issues huh?" he asked with a smile.

Trey flashed a smile back at him, leaned against the desk, and ran a hand through his hair, or tried to. His fingers snagged on a knot.

"You, er..." Conor gestured. "You have a little... can I just...?" He reached out tentatively and plucked a leaf from Trey's hair. The position brought him close. "There. All fixed." Warmth touched Conor's face. He drew back and looked for somewhere to deposit the leaf before deciding to set it beside a roll of parchment.

"I had a run-in with some thieves."

Conor's deep brown eyes widened. "Ah, you're the messenger Venali saved. We heard about that." The male gave him a second, more thorough visual assessment that ended in a raised eyebrow, making Trey question exactly what Venali had said.

Being *saved* by Venali made it sound like he'd been some helpless elfling alone on the moors rescued by the dashing sentinel.

Trey cleared his throat. "I was saving myself before Venali showed up."

"That's not how he told it," Conor muttered, cheeks warming some more. He concentrated on emptying the packages and letters, logging each one and its recipient on his parchment. His attention elsewhere, Trey stole a moment to admire Conor and his physique more suitable to manual labor than file shuffling. His warm skin tones suggested Conor enjoyed long periods outside in the sun. The warmth stayed with him out of the sun, too, and Trey found himself wondering if the male's blushing and long glances were an indication of more than a casual interest. One he might be open to exploring later.

"Do you have somewhere I can get cleaned up?" Trey asked.

"Of course. We have lodgings set aside for you." Conor produced a wooden key and slid it across the desk. "You'll find things have much improved since your last stay. We have hot running water and we're working on a supply of electricity, but until then, our lights are all oil-fueled, so please do ventilate your room by opening a window. Thank you for your messenger service, Trey. It really is appreciated." Conor smiled again, warming Trey through. "We'll have another delivery ready for you in two days. Do you know how to get to the residential area?"

"Yes, thank you. And I'll maybe see you 'round Ashford before I leave?"

Conor's gaze heated too. "I'd like that."

Trey pushed off the desk, body thrumming warmly now that he was in the safety of Ashford and its people. He sauntered through the sunlit, main atrium, soaking up the warmth and heat before heading deeper into Ashford.

Previously blocked off doorways and floors had been opened, linked by open-plan staircases and landings. Signs pointed to trading areas and council chambers, recreational zones, and various other gathering places. Ashford had tripled in size. Now that the settlement's existence was widely known, more elves had moved in. Traders' stalls had sprung up in some of the larger alcoves.

Trey found the residential block and let another admin helper lead him to his room. The window was the first thing he noticed, and then the light spilling inside, filling the space. All windows had been blocked up before. All but the main atrium's glass ceiling, and even that had been half-hidden behind shrubs.

In a small side room, he found the bathing and toilet facilities and tested the water, finding it remarkably warm. He climbed into a closet, the type he'd heard humans call a shower, and marveled at the feel of hot water washing over him. After weeks on the road, a waterfall of warm water was a luxury he could get used to.

Skin tingling and steaming, he dried off, wrapped the towel around his waist, and emerged from the bathroom to find a dragonblade dagger stabbed into the inside of the main door, holding a note in place.

Someone had been in his room.

His own blade still rested on the bed next to his unpacked bag. Nothing had been disturbed.

He pulled the dagger free of the door and opened the note.

> *Midnight at the library.*
> *Bring the blade.*

The dagger was a fine piece of work, clearly an Order blade. He frowned at the blade and note. Padding barefoot back to the bed, he tossed the dagger onto the top sheet next to his own sword.

Daggers and notes? This wasn't an official Order summons. This was something else. Something *interesting*. Trey smiled.

NOBODY SEEMED to know Ashford had a library, and with no signs to point the way, Trey headed toward the entryway desk to ask Conor. A helpful female told him Conor was off-shift, but she reeled off directions to *the library* with something of a strange, knowing smile, leading him deeper into the heart of old-Ashford.

Libraries were meant for books and quiet contemplation.

Trey had heard that much about them. Although, he'd never actually set foot in one. There weren't enough books left in the world to warrant rooms dedicated to them. But the room he approached down the end of a corridor wasn't quiet. Behind a stocky male blocking the way, he caught sight of oil lamps glowing in nooks. Racks of shelves that may have once held books now held rows of colored glass items, bottles and bowls, most broken at one time and haphazardly fixed together with tape and glue. When the flickering light from the oil lamps hit the strange ornaments, colors danced on the walls. Music flowed, too, just enough to tempt Trey forward.

A boulder of a male stepped into his path and grunted, "Blade?"

Trey handed over the dagger and underwent a head to toe assessment. The guard grumbled, "I'll see this gets back to its owner," before nodding Trey through.

Laughter peppered the air. Trey's nose twitched at the sweet smell of wine and incense. A small group of musicians played a lively tune, brightening the atmosphere, making toes tap, automatically lifting Trey's lips into a smile.

He'd only managed a few steps when someone planted a cup of something into his hand, patted him on the shoulder, and moved off through the crowd before Trey could thank them.

He tasted the wine, finding it sweet and strong. He really could get used to this. Drifting about, he caught a few curious glances cast his way, most female, some male. All wore their Order blades, blades that had been soaked in dragon blood, blades no longer needed in a time of peace. He raised the cup to his lips and drank deep, beginning to understand the draw of such a place to those like him. Every single soul here was an Order assassin. They had lived and breathed and dreamed killing for as long as they could remember. Trey wasn't entirely like them, he hadn't been raised to kill dragons, but he felt a kinship all the same.

His cup ran dry too soon, but he'd ambled to the bar by chance. The female pouring drinks noticed his empty cup and waved him over.

"You're the messenger," the female at the bar grinned, taking his cup and refilling it from her jug.

"I don't have payment, but I—"

"All assassins already paid." She winked. "Trey, isn't it?"

There had to be almost seventy elves here and she'd recognized him among them and under the shifting light? "Am I that obvious?"

"A few of us saw you arrive. Saw you with Eroan at the battle too. You were part of Eroan's pride. Ashford would be nothing but ash without your assistance. A better question is who doesn't know you." She offered her hand. "Kalie."

He shook, humbled and slightly uncomfortable with the praise. He'd just done the same as any elf would. He'd done what was right. "So, what is this place? It doesn't appear to be much of a library."

"But it is *something*." She filled a few more cups and sent her patrons off with a genuine smile. "This is a safe place for retired blades." She picked up a towel and wiped a cup clean, her hands working fast with familiarity. Her blond hair was cropped short into a bob. She wore it tucked behind her tipped ears, showing off an impressive collection of trinket earrings. Tattoos like Trey's snaked down her neck and shoulder, traveling beneath her thin-sleeved top. Cheen elves marked themselves that way to remember the lost. Hers looked recent.

"Did you skewer the note to my door?" he asked.

Her grin turned sly. "Could have been any one of us. We look after our own and we couldn't have you spending the night alone."

Trey scanned the crowd, recognizing faces he'd fought alongside. Without dragons to kill, elves who had trained their entire lives to bring them down suddenly found themselves without a purpose. He knew what that felt like, hence falling back into wandering. But most of these assassins had nothing else to fall back on. So clearly they came here, and as the musician's music grew louder, they led their partners to a small, clear area and danced to the toe-tapping music. Others found comfort in company and wine. He briefly wondered what Eroan would think of such a place. When he'd first met Eroan, he'd have loved a place like this, but the assassin had hardened over the years. They all had. Still, lately, Eroan had brightened again. He'd approve of this place. Trey's teacher, Nye, would not have.

Trey offered his cup for a third or fourth refill, hoping the alcoholic haze might smudge away some of the more painful memories.

"We'll have you dancing in no time," Kalie said.

He hadn't danced in... months. He might yet be persuaded, with more wine. He lifted the cup to Kalie. "To the Order."

Kalie picked her own glass up and chinked it with Trey's, then downed her wine in one gulp, barely wincing. "You must get around as a messenger, huh? All those different places, different folks too..." A mischievous glint made her eyes shine. She leaned in, fixing Trey beneath her sultry gaze. "I heard you messengers pick up all kinds of *talents* from your travels."

"Oh, we do." He leaned closer too. It had been a while since he'd played loose and free with his *desires*. Working as a messenger had allowed him a great deal of sexual freedom. Maybe it was time to take up that pursuit again, but not with Kalie. Lowering his voice, he added, "If females were my preference, I'd show you exactly the kind of talents I've collected."

"Well, damn." She pouted, but her smile quickly sprang back.

"I'll take you up on that dance later, though," he said.

"I'd like that."

A ripple passed through the room, flowing outward from the main door like a bow wave. Trey felt the shift in the atmosphere as much as saw it on the faces of the crowd. A pride of three had arrived, already laughing and sprawled over one another. At their center, the star they revolved around was Sentinel Venali. Trey had to look twice to be sure this was the same stern, reserved male he'd seen on the battlefield and on the moor. He wore layers of autumn reds and golden browns, the clothes tailored to fit like a second skin, high-lighting a long, lean frame. His waistcoat was a delight of embroidered red roses against black cotton. He said some-thing to the female hooked under his arm, making her laugh aloud. Mirth animated his face, made him come alive and shine. He knew how to attract the attention of everyone in the room, and he clearly reveled in it.

As Trey watched, a male peeled from the crowd, clutched Venali's face in both hands, and kissed him long and deep. This was no chaste kiss of friendship. Venali threaded his fingers into the male's hair, clutching him close and devoured him where he stood, kissing him like they were both starved of the other.

"Close your mouth, Trey." Kalie snorted.

Heat warmed Trey's face. He turned away and downed the wine in one gulp, catching Kalie's knowing smirk.

"I hear you know Venali," she said, clearly fishing for more.

"We met." Every cell in Trey's body ached to turn, to see, to watch the commotion behind him. He could hear their laughter and raucous behavior and a part of him wanted to be among it—the old, free-loving, careless part of him that went away during the war, or maybe before then, when he'd stopped wandering.

The atmosphere crackled, the crowd getting louder to match Venali's ego. Even the band seemed to sense the change and switched their music to a faster, brighter beat.

"Bit of a shock, huh? You'll find him quite different when he's not working," Kalie explained, lining up three fresh cups.

Trey glanced back. Venali had lost the male he'd used his tongue to examine but had gathered a small crowd around him. He talked and laughed and gestured as though utterly at ease with an audience. "I can see that."

"We each have our way of coping," Kalie quietly added, like an after-thought.

Venali extracted himself from the grip of his companions and sauntered over, walking like he knew every person in the room admired him.

Trey briefly found his cup fascinating, fighting not to fall into the same spell as everyone else here and just *look*. He was fucking gorgeous.

"Sentinel." Kalie reached beneath her countertop and brought out a green bottle of something dark. "Look what I found rattling around the archives."

Venali made an appreciative humming sound that apparently had a direct link to Trey's much-neglected cock. This was not the time or place for such thoughts and certainly not with a raging self-centered prick like Venali. Trey focused on a knot in a wooden support beam, diverting his thoughts far away.

"Kalie, darling... Did you steal it from Alador?" the male purred.

On the moor, Venali's tone had been rock-hard and unforgiving. It still held that same hardened edge now, but with an added grumbling purr that rumbled through Trey and made him acutely aware of the sentinel's powerful presence beside him. He didn't even like the asshole.

"As if I would do such a thing, sentinel!" Kalie dumped the bottle on the counter. "On the house, for finally tracking those murdering bastards down."

"Much obliged, Kalie." The bottle was gone and Trey figured he'd escaped without being seen until the weight of Venali's gaze landed on him. His skin prickled. Maybe he didn't have to look, maybe he could just ignore him and he'd go away.

Trey looked.

Elves didn't have magic, but Venali had *something*, and now Trey was snared in Venali's ocean-green eyes, unable and unwilling to break free. Long auburn lashes framed the kind of eyes that saw everything.

"Did you bury them?" Venali asked, leaning a hip against the bar.

"Yeah." Trey lifted his chin, trying to scrabble around his own thoughts for something else to say, but the longer he delayed, the more Venali's attention set his veins ablaze. And the more Trey's heart raced, the more annoyed he grew. Was this asshole just going to stare at him all night? If he was trying to shame him for doing the right thing, he'd be waiting a long time.

Trey stared back, deliberately skewering Venali with his own kind of stare, pinning it to his face. If he hadn't, his attention might have roamed over the male's figure, drinking him in like a glass of cool water on a hot summer day, admiring how that fine waistcoat tucked in around a thin waist. He wore gloves, Trey noticed, and now thinking back, he'd seen him wear what looked to be the same gloves on the moor. Supple leather fit snugly around long, careful fingers. *Fuck*. Trey's cock twitched.

"Did you bury them for you or them?" Venali asked.

The question tripped Trey's thoughts over. Before he could think of an answer, Venali pushed away, raised the bottle to a wave of appreciative howls, and fell among his adoring people. His entourage swallowed him up, and Trey let out a breath.

With Venali gone, the background music and laughter trickled back in. Venali's attention had made it seem as though, for those few moments, they'd been alone. Clearing his throat, he turned toward the bar. Getting hard in public for any pretty face and a honey-smooth voice? If someone like Venali was turning his blood hot, he really needed to get laid.

"Venali's intense," Kalie said. Her raised eyebrow suggested she might be fishing for a reaction.

"That's one word for him." Trey had too much gravel in his voice. Alumn, it really had been too long.

She poked her tongue into her cheek and nodded toward the rowdy group. "Venali is... complicated."

"No shit."

"It's just—"

"Thanks for the drinks, Kalie. And for the invite." He left his glass at the bar and headed for the door. With any luck, he could slip out, go take a cold shower, and call it a night.

Then the musicians started playing a fast, jolly tune. A young male voice rose above the conversation, singing about a girl on her wedding day, and almost half the crowd moved to the dance area, arms looped together, boots tapping against the hard floor. Hands clapped, and a flute player started up, joined by the fiddle.

Trey's pace toward the door slowed.

Some in the crowd took up the singer's words, joining in with him, and Trey's torn and battered heart lifted. So maybe he could stay a little while. He'd be on the road again soon, and as much as he enjoyed the quiet, he needed company too.

He'd once played hard in every settlement he'd passed through because, in those days, the next day might be his last. Now, he wasn't as likely to die on the treks between villages, but a part of him still ached for that careless thrill of no commitment or responsibility.

"Leaving so soon?" Conor emerged from the crowd. His smile was the same warm, inviting grin he'd worn at the desk, but now the wine had added a dash of heat to his cheeks. Brown eyes captured the shifting light, warming those too.

A sense of relief at Conor's company cinched it. He'd been alone too long. This was exactly what he needed. "Not just yet."

"Wanna dance?" Conor blurted, wine making him bold.

"Always."

The next few hours passed in a blur of song and dance and wine, so much wine, and with every hour, Conor's touches grew more adventurous, migrating from Trey's shoulder to his thigh, and later, pressed against a wall, hands on Trey's ass, tongue teasing, luring him deeper. Alumn, it felt good to be free again. To not be tied down by responsibility. He'd spent too long in the Order, too long fighting, he needed simple pleasures.

Conor had found some corner of the library and tucked them out of sight from much of the crowd. He'd pulled Trey into it, but it was Trey who pinned the male to the wall, held his wrists at his sides, and lavished the kind of attention on him that would surely see them get thrown out if they were seen.

Trey cared little for rules. He wasn't planning on sticking around, and by the time he next came back around to Ashford, they'd likely have forgotten about any indiscretions. Messengers were always wanted. If Trey fucked Conor right here against the wall, it would probably be overlooked. Besides, there were others here not nearly as discreet. "We should go somewhere..." Conor whispered, his breath hot in Trey's ear.

"Right here is just fine." Trey plastered himself against Conor's body, relishing the feel of male hardness against his own, and not just his cock. Trey had been right, Conor's body was a map of hard muscle and lean strength, honed from physical work.

"We're doing this... right here?" Conor asked, sounding equal parts appalled and aroused.

Trey freed one of Conor's wrists and dropped his hand to press against Conor's impressive erection. The male groaned and tilted his hips, inviting more of Trey's harsh caress. Trey's own arousal was raging hard and demanding. It had been too long since he'd enjoyed the personal company of another. His last bedmate had been Nye—his Order leader—and that... that hadn't ended well.

"You ever fucked in public?" Trey whispered, nipping at Conor's jaw. "The thrill of almost getting caught?" He rubbed Conor's cock through his trouser fabric, shortening the male's every breath. "I'll get you off right here. You can bet we're being watched. What do you say we give them a show?"

"Shit," Conor's grip found Trey's shoulder and dug in. "*Venali*," he hissed.

Trey leaned outward and scanned the crowd, initially not seeing what had Conor spooked. And then when he did see him, he couldn't look away fast enough.

Venali's green eyes fixed on Trey's from across the room. Sprawled in a chair, legs spread, Venali smiled and tipped his cup, as though giving them *permission* to continue their display just for him.

"He's making me nervous. I can't..." Conor breathed.

Maybe they should take this somewhere else, but if they did that, Venali would have won, and it seemed every time Trey met or spoke with Venali, Venali won.

Trey caught Conor's jaw and tore his attention from Venali. Conor's kissable mouth quirked. His hand found Trey's ass, drawing him close so there was nothing between them but the press of too many clothes. His fingers dug in deep, catching Trey's breath. Now this was more like it. Trey kissed him hard, driving his tongue in. Conor's rumbling purr strummed Trey's lust. It had to be the purr, because the lust couldn't be from how Venali's gaze rode Trey's back while Trey's hand rode Conor's cock.

The male panted beneath him, coming undone, and Trey was more than happy to unravel him some more. He'd have preferred to go down on him with his mouth and tongue, but even Trey had some limits, and while he didn't have to live with these people and see them every day, Conor did. He may not appreciate a public blow come the morning once the wine had worn off.

Conor dropped his head back, inviting Trey's mouth to his neck. "Alumn, you feel so good."

Trey rewarded the words with a purr of his own.

Venali's attention heated Trey to his bones. He stole a glance, and there he was, still lounged in the chair. Someone leaned close to him, speaking in his ear, but Venali still watched. Trey roamed his gaze down the male's chest, beyond where his waistcoat bunched, to where the male's hard rod of a cock pushed against his crotch.

Lust sparked down Trey's back. He bit his lip to keep from groaning. It wasn't enough. Fuck, Venali was hot. But the male's *"complicated"* dick was absolutely off-limits. Trey needed easy. Not... whatever Venali was.

Trey plundered Conor's mouth hard. His heart tried to hammer its way out of his chest. His cock throbbed, needing attention, either from his own hand, Conor's, or to be thrust into some other part of Conor, but despite Trey's inhibitions, he wasn't about to turn the male around and fuck him here.

Even drunk, he had some control left. But he could get him off. And Venali could fucking watch all he liked.

Unthreading Conor's pant ties, Trey eased his hand inside, grateful to find Conor's crown slick with pre-seed. The male swore in his ear, clutched Trey close, and shuddered his pleasure. Conor's hips twitched, his body's demands clear. Trey smothered Conor's groan with a kiss, and sealed his fingers and thumb around Conor's pulsing cock, stroking him off with smooth, rhythmic pumps. Venali was fucking watching and some animal part of Trey needed him to.

Conor's breaths stuttered. Trey smothered his mouth, thrusting his tongue in as the male came, his seed hot and wet against his palm. The kiss was messy and rough, a tangle of tongues and teeth, but Alumn, he tasted sweet. Conor's hand had found its way to Trey's hair and bunched it in a fist some time in all the madness. He let it drop now and rested his head back, swallowing hard. "Did he see?"

Trey furtively checked over his shoulder. Venali had gone. Maybe he'd gone off somewhere to deal with his own hard-on. Disappointment cooled Trey's lust, and then sparked alive the feeling that he was a fucking idiot to seek any kind of attention from an attention whore like Venali.

"Maybe. He's gone now."

Conor's fingers groped for Trey's trouser laces.

"Whoa there..." Trey nudged his cheek with his nose and whispered, "I'm good."

"You don't want to?"

The hurt in his voice made Trey straighten and study his face. Emotive brown eyes told a raw story of wanting. Trey stroked a thumb across his cheek. "I do, but let's go somewhere..."

"Come back to my place with me?" Conor asked, nipping at Trey's bottom lip.

The offer was tempting. He'd slept alone enough. Waking

next to a lover was one of the few joys left in life. But there was an art to the one-night seduction, and Conor had a need in his touch, his kiss, that spoke of wanting more. And more was not on the table. It couldn't be.

"Is it Venali?"

"What? No. Why would he—"

A tinny bell chimed. It wasn't loud, but its pitch sliced through the music. The crowd erupted like a flock of startled birds.

"Shit!" Conor grabbed Trey's hand, yanked him out of the nook, and shoved him into a tatty old armchair.

"What—"

"Act natural." Conor plucked a book from a nearby shelf, dropped into the chair beside Trey's, and apparently found his book absolutely fascinating, despite it being upside down.

"Alador," a chipper voice said from the doorway. "Lovely to see you here, sir."

Trey jerked his head up.

The Order leader entered the "library" and scanned the now sedate crowd apparently all lounged about reading or chatting quietly, certainly not drinking or fucking or dancing to music played by musicians who had apparently dissolved into the crowd as though they were never here.

Alador was as old as Ashford's tree. He'd seen the rise of the dragons and their fall. As the first assassin, he'd practically invented the Order. He was also a father figure to most everyone in the Order.

Trey figured Alador's sudden arrival was like having your pa find you with your cock in your fist.

"Fuck," Trey whispered. Conor snickered. Spotting a ratty, half torn book on the floor, Trey scooped it up and pretended to be engrossed in its grubby, nonsensical pages. He didn't even recognize the language.

Alador drifted about the room, talking to a few elves.

Trey sunk lower in the chair, listening to the elder draw closer. At least Venali's leaving had deflated more than his mood.

"Ah, Trey! It's good to see you again. How is Eroan?"

Trey lowered the book and plastered a broad smile on his face. He stood and dipped his head. "I'm honored to be here. Eroan is finding new worlds to explore."

"Not too far, I hope." The old elf's brow crinkled. "We can't have the dragons untethered for long."

"Not far, no."

The elder's dark hair had been pinned back from his face, but allowed to flow free over his shoulders and down his back. In his robes, he appeared very different now to how Trey had last seen him, wrapped in battle leathers and bristling with blades. But he hadn't lost the hard, wily look of someone who had seen all the shit and was immune to surprise.

"I don't believe I properly thanked you for your service," Alador said. "Will you do me the honor of walking in the sun with me. Perhaps tomorrow?"

"Of course."

Alador dipped his chin and smiled, but hesitated a moment before moving on. In that moment between moments, Trey got the distinct impression Alador knew exactly what went on here, but for the sake of appearances, couldn't get involved or be seen to condone it.

He moved on to a pair beside Trey and spoke to them about some new venture on Ashford's outskirts. Trey slipped his hand in Conor's and pulled him to his feet, hastily walking him from the library.

Conor quickly fell into fits of laughter. "Your face when he singled you out…" They hurried down a shadowy side corridor, heading the long route that Trey hoped would eventually wind its way back to the atrium.

25

"You could have warned me! What if he'd walked in on us earlier?"

Conor snickered and stumbled, clinging onto Trey's arm. "He doesn't always come around. Someone probably told him you were there."

"Someone like Venali?" And Venali had chosen a time when Trey might have embarrassed himself in front of Ashford's elder. Was that deliberate?

"Maybe. Venali is so far up Alador's ass, it's unreal."

"What's his problem—?" They rounded a corner and came upon Venali leaning a shoulder against the wall, hand tucked into a pocket, looking like he'd been there all night and had nothing to do with Alador's unscheduled visit.

He held a cup craned in his gloved fingers at his side. A drunken gleam made his green eyes shimmer. "What's my problem with what?"

"With me," Trey said, ignoring how a shock of lust reignited his veins. Him just leaning there, with his perfect clothes and haughty persona. It made Trey want to punch him, or kiss him. Alumn, what would kissing him be like?

"Who said I had a problem with you?" Venali raised the cup and took a drink, making his graceful neck pulse.

He had to know exactly the effect he had on others, else why dress like a gift waiting to be unwrapped. He'd certainly known how to play to a crowd. Where were they now? All his Venali devotees?

"C'mon," Trey ventured closer, overstepping personal space. "You've been on my ass since the moor. Was it because I showed those thieves some respect or something else?"

Venali tipped his cup toward Trey. "I am most definitely not on your ass." Venali's gaze skipped down and back up, no more than a flicker. He'd brazenly checked out Trey's ass, undressing him with his eyes.

Heat touched Trey's face. He hated this prick, he really

did, but also wanted to jump his elegant bones and hate-fuck him so hard against the wall right now.

"C'mon..." Conor mumbled, taking a wide arc around Venali, treating him like a wild animal about to lunge at any second.

Trey followed, keeping Venali in the corner of his eye until passing him. Walking away wasn't so hard. Even if another, more demanding part of his anatomy really was. The sentinel had some kind of direct link to Trey's cock, making the damn thing dance with just a smirk and a raised eyebrow.

They'd almost made it to the next corner when Venali said, "A bit early to retire, isn't it?"

Conor turned and glanced at Trey, an unspoken question on his lips, one that seemed to ask if Trey had heard the same invite in the sentinel's tone.

Venali hadn't moved. He still leaned against the wall, his ego taking up the entire corridor.

He finished his drink, pushed off the wall, and strode in the opposite direction. Considering how drunk he had to be, he carried a swagger that advertised a body designed from the ground up to either kill professionally or fuck like an animal, or both. Maybe he wasn't drunk at all and the glimmer in his eyes was more predatory than intoxication. Alumn, what a thought that was.

Conor shrugged. "He, er... I mean, I guess we could follow... if you want to?"

What kind of game was Venali playing here? And if they went with him, what were they agreeing to exactly? Trey's rampant desires had a good idea but common sense held him back. Kalie had said Venali was complicated. Trey was done with complicated. And yet...

There wasn't a challenge Trey hadn't beaten. Venali was just another challenge, something to distract him and make the next few days entertaining before he got back on the road.

Trey put one foot in front of the other and found it far too easy to trail after Venali, Conor in tow. They caught up with Venali's long strides and walked in silence until reaching a door Trey assumed led to Venali's residential space.

Venali flicked over the lock and entered, leaving the door open as an invitation. He lit a few oil lamps, filling the space with warm, flickering light. Clearly, Venali really was up Alador's ass, because the room was easily five times the size of Trey's allocated lodgings, with a wall of windows over-looking a swathe of darkness that during the day was likely the meadow outside Ashford. Now the wall of black reflected Venali's cat-like grace as he crossed the room. He dumped his cup on a table and began unbuttoning his waistcoat. His gloved fingers worked quickly, precisely.

Conor clicked the door closed.

"Nice place," Trey said, needing to say something.

Venali either didn't hear or didn't care to. He shrugged off the waistcoat and draped it over the arm of one of two large couches. He worked at the shirt next, but unbuttoned just the collar, letting it gape open, revealing a tantalizing glimpse of more.

Trey still wasn't entirely sure what this was. It was unlikely Venali had asked him here to talk. That left mostly sex. One of those options was more appealing than the other.

"You're from Cheen?" Venali asked.

Trey narrowed his eyes. "How did you know—"

He swept his gloved fingers at his own neck, echoing the path of Trey's tattoos. "You lost someone?" he asked, recognizing the significance of the marks.

"Someone." *Everyone.*

Conor drifted about the large, open room, admiring mirrors and salvaged cupboards, tables and chairs. Trinkets of an old world, either repurposed or reconfigured into new items of furniture. Had Venali crafted them himself with those delicate fingers of his?

He still wore the gloves. Maybe to hide scars? Or maybe he just didn't like to touch, although he'd been happy enough to touch those of his pride, like the male he'd kissed on arriving at the library.

"Where's your partner?"

Venali looked up. "My what?"

"The male from the library?"

"You'll have to narrow it down." The sly smirk said he knew exactly who Trey referred to.

"The male you were *pleased* to see."

"Oh, him. He's not my partner." He dismissed with a wave, and then took a corked bottle from a cupboard, along with three cups. He filled the cups, handing one out to Conor.

"Do you kiss all acquaintances like that?" Trey asked.

Venali's hard mouth found its wry smile again. "Some."

Clearing his throat, Trey loosened off his jacket, found a hook on the paneled wall, and hung it. When he turned, Venali was suddenly too close, holding out the drink.

"You have a new tattoo?" the sentinel asked.

"Thanks." Trey took the drink and reeled from the question. How did Venali know Trey had recently added more ink? "I do." He wasn't saying anymore, not to Venali. Even Eroan didn't know why Trey had added more dark swirls to the pattern climbing his neck. Some things didn't need to be said aloud.

He tasted the drink, found it burned pleasantly on his tongue, and swallowed deep, letting it warm his veins. Conor had gotten comfortable on the couch, rolling up his sleeves and taking eager sips of his drink like he needed the courage.

"It must be a hard life, being a messenger," Venali said,

returning to the couch to look down at Conor.

Conor's throat bobbed. He wilted some beneath Venali's presence looming over him.

"Easier now dragons are tamed."

"Still, there are other monsters hiding in the dark, like the two I killed. You're welcome, by the way, for saving your life."

Trey's pride bristled. "I had it in hand."

"You could have retired from the Order," Venali went on. "Made a home with someone. Instead, you went back to the road. You like it." Despite looking down at Conor, the words were clearly meant for Trey. "No ties, no roots, no strings." He reached out and tipped Conor's chin up. "I appreciate the freedom in that."

Trey saw Conor's pulse fluttering from across the room and felt his own race in empathy, or maybe it was racing because he imagined sitting on the couch with Venali standing over him, the male's fingers stroking his jaw, his mouth a kissable promise.

Trey's eager cock was already in the game and had been since Venali had watched him get Conor off in the library, but now it muddled Trey's thoughts, made him see where this dance was going.

Venali combed his gloved fingers into Conor's hair and the male leaned into the touch, lips parting. It was no happy accident Conor happened to be sitting and Venali standing, putting Conor at exactly the same height as Venali's crotch, Conor's mouth inches from the rod upsetting the line of Venali's dark trousers.

Alumn, it was hot in here. Trey set his drink on the side and loosened off the laces tying his shirt closed. He missed something Conor said but heard Venali's soft reply, "... safe." Goddess, Conor looked at Venali like he'd sell his soul to the next dragon to suck Venali off right now. Alumn, Trey might do the same to watch them.

Watching so wasn't Trey. But neither was Venali. He'd do this, to scratch an itch, but he wasn't about to fawn over Venali like some besotted elfling just because Venali happened to look like sex-on-legs. He clearly had his head so far up his own ass he could lick his own balls.

Venali downed his drink, set the empty cup on the side table beside the couch, and began to unbutton his shirt.

Conor couldn't have looked more desperate if he started drooling. He hadn't looked at Trey like that in the library.

Trey liked to think of himself as something of a professional when it came to pleasure. He'd been around, visited more than a few beds in each settlement he'd passed through, learned some tricks along the way. Sure, it had been a few years since those escapades, but he still had it in him. At least, he'd thought so, until Venali. Now he felt like some damn virgin hovering on the outskirts while Venali and Conor eye-fucked each other.

Venali pulled his shirt off and tossed it aside, catching Trey's intense glare in the process. Lust sizzled low, stealing any pretense of control.

Venali crooked a gloved finger, like Trey was some pet to be summoned. Heat pulsed through Trey's cock, clearly happy to oblige. He took a step forward. Whatever happened, when he woke tomorrow, he could blame it on the drink. Another step. Then another, bringing him close to Venali's naked back. His smooth skin held a golden sheen, the kind Trey ached to bite, especially those muscular shoulders and arms.

Venali looked down at Conor again. His back flexed, lean and powerful. Trey moved before he'd thought ahead and swept Venali's hair up in a knot around his fist, holding it firm. No longer able to resist, he bowed his head and tasted the curve of Venali's neck, stroking his tongue over one tiny spot and then sucking gently, pinching the skin between his teeth.

31

Venali shivered. "Yes."

Maybe he said yes for Conor, Trey almost didn't care. He tasted like sunlight and something spiced and warming. Trey swirled his tongue, wanting more, and nipped lower, biting at the male's shoulder.

Venali lifted his head, resting it back, allowing Trey to nuzzle behind his ear and flick his tongue along the edge of Venali's tapered ear. Venali moaned. Lust spritzed Trey's skin. He could go back to hating Venali when this was over, but right now he needed him, needed to feel this coldhearted, powerful bastard shudder beneath his touch and beg for more. Trey usually preferred the more submissive role, but not for this sentinel. There was no way he was bending for him.

Trey dropped his hands to Venali's hips, feeling Venali's twitching. The male's trouser waist had already dropped an inch over his hips, likely due to Conor loosening off his fly. Trey pushed them farther down, sliding the belt over Venali's rounded ass and then palmed both buttocks, digging his thumbs in, caressing and kneading the warm, pert skin as he swirled and kissed a path down Venali's back.

Alumn, Venali had a body meant for worshipping. Trey had known it. He'd seen it months ago when they'd fought in the same battle, and saw it again on the moor when Venali had fired his arrows and killed the bandits, but to taste and bite and dig his fingers into that silken hardness was more than he could have imagined. He couldn't get enough, and yet strangely, it *was* enough.

Conor's hand reached around and opened and nudged Trey's thigh for attention. His fingers opened, revealing a small pot of oily cream. Whatever it was originally meant for, Trey quickly gathered its new purpose.

He dug his fingers into the slippery cream while kissing his way up Venali's spine, then pushed his middle finger down the valley of Venali's ass, sinking it deeper until finding that tightly rippled circle of muscle. Gently probing made Venali arch his shoulders back and drive his ass toward Trey's finger, his need obvious. Trey suckled Venali's shoulder and circled his finger some more, delicately approaching the center, but as Venali's groans grew ragged, he eased his finger into the puckered ring. He was damned tight. Too tight.

"Relax," Trey whispered, easing his finger in and out in a quick beat, not going deep, deliberately avoiding the spot he knew Venali wanted him to stroke. As willing as Venali clearly was, penetrating too soon would hurt and no amount of lubricant was going to ease that.

Venali's breaths raced, his body a writhing thing in Trey's hands. Conor was clearly working on his cock and Trey felt that little nudge of jealousy again. He couldn't do it all, and right now, he was content enough preparing Venali's ass, because he planned to own it as soon as Venali was ready.

"Strip," Venali ordered, but not to Trey. Conor stood, catching Trey's eye over Venali's shoulder. They had the sentinel trapped between them, Trey's finger was well-placed in the male's hole while Conor likely had his hand on Venali's erection. The lust aglow in Conor's eyes was a whole new level of pleasure, making Trey growl with need. He stretched Venali open, easing in a second finger, making him grunt and clench. This time Trey did stroke forward, caressing that puckered nub.

"Fuck!" the sentinel gasped.

Then Conor was turning around and bracing himself over the couch, his naked back glistening beneath the lick of oil light.

Trey looped an arm around Venali's neck, catching the sentinel off guard. Venali had Conor spread and wet before him, and now Trey had Venali locked against his chest. "You want this?" Trey asked, trying to whisper and utterly failing. He'd growled the words.

He stroked his finger inward, running his fingertips over the nub of nerves inside Venali's passage. The sentinel's hips tilted, his cock would be poised against Conor's ass, but it was Trey who held them both back.

"Say it," Trey growled. "I have to hear you say the word."

"Yes," Venali hissed, like he hated it, him and everything happening, but consented anyway.

Trey freed him. Venali shuddered and grabbed Conor's hips with one hand, his own cock with the other. Venali's ass clenched as he pushed himself into Conor's hole. Conor spat a curse and arched, thrusting his ass back, stealing another gasp from Venali.

Trey had watched enough. He tore his own fly laces loose and freed his neglected erection, stroking some of the lube around the crown and giving himself a few greedy strokes.

Still dressed, there was no need to strip off, he had what he wanted spread open and puckered up. Venali was too damn tight still, but Trey eased in, rolling his eyes as that sweet, slippery tightness enveloped him, inch by careful inch. Venali grunted. It was the sweetest damn sound he'd heard in months.

Trey eased out and pushed in. He did the same again, losing his grip on his fast unraveling control. And then Venali began to thrust into Conor, rocking back onto Trey's cock, spilling waves of pleasure through him. He'd been ready to grip Venali's hips and take him hard, but having Venali set the pace switched Trey's mind to a whole other level of wrecked. Venali's hole sucked on him, like tight, hot lips, and it was all Trey could do to hold onto some control.

Conor's see-saw breaths came faster than Venali's, who seemed to have a better rein on himself, although he was slipping free too.

Perspiration gleamed across Venali's golden shoulders and dripped down his spine. Trey stroked his thumb up the slick muscles, digging in deep, making sure Venali knew whose cock pulsed into him.

Conor's panting grew tighter, faster, pleasure about to trip him over the edge. Trey clutched at Venali's hips, easing himself out of the maddening rhythm before the sounds of Conor losing his seed triggered the same in Trey. He was close too.

"Fuck!" Conor shuddered. Venali clutched at his thighs and thrust hard, once, twice, slapping skin against skin. Trey staggered back a step, keeping his hands well away from his own erect and twitching member. It wouldn't take much to come, a few more strokes, a few more images of Venali thrusting hilt deep into Conor's ass, making Conor choke out his grunts, and Trey would be lost.

Venali held Conor down, his hand spread on his back, fiercely claiming. He was lost now, his lips pulled back into a sneer, his body arched over Conor, hips pumping mindlessly. He came hard, tight ass clenching, thrusting forward, teeth gritted. Alumn, Venali was raw and hard and more animal than elf, and Trey was so close to bursting, he was going to lose it without another touch.

Venali whirled suddenly and came at Trey like a wolf attacking its prey. The sudden approach drove Trey stumbling backward. He hit a wall and then Venali was on him, his mouth forcing his open, his tongue thrusting and taking. His gloved hand gripped Trey's swollen cock and it was too much all at once. Pleasure snapped free, jerking Trey's hips and tearing a cry from his smothered mouth. He came so damn hard he might have fallen if Venali hadn't been holding him pinned against the wall. Pulses freed his seed all over Venali's fine gloves, smoothing Venali's thumb as he brushed Trey's tip. Pleasure turned to oversensitive pain, making Trey hiss.

And then Venali backed off, splendid in his flushed nakedness, his cock semi-hard and his blue-green eyes alight with ecstasy.

He chuckled, the sound sending pleasurable after-pulses through Trey's cock, and turned away to beckon Conor to follow him.

Trey watched, breathless and numb, as Conor hurried after him through a door Trey presumed to be a bedroom. Moments later, the sound of water hissed an invitation from behind that door.

Trey puffed out a heavy breath and dragged a hand down his face. He felt wrecked, like he'd had his soul set ablaze. And he felt something else, too, like maybe he'd like more of what Venali gave, but then wouldn't he be just like the others hanging onto Venali's arm, like the male Venali had kissed in the library? Trey was not falling into that come-hither trick with someone who clearly cared more about themselves than anyone else.

He'd sated that urge, and after tucking himself away, he scooped his coat off the hook and left.

PAIN THUMPED behind his eyes and down the back of his neck. Trey wanted to bury himself beneath the sheets until the next dispatch was due. Too much of whatever Venali had given him to drink mixed with wine. But he distinctly recalled agreeing to walk in the sun with Alador and the elder was not someone you stood up.

He showered again, dressed in fresh clothes, and headed for the atrium only to find Venali and Alador already there, deep in conversation. Apparently, this was *working Venali*. He didn't spare a glance at Trey. Wrapped up in the same Ashford-sigil-marked leathers as when they'd met on the moor, he was back to being the rod-up-his-ass sentinel he'd always been. Except, Trey's rod had been up his ass. Trey delighted in recalling that memory now, using it to fuel a smile as he closed in on the pair.

"Trey," Alador greeted. "Walk with me, it's a glorious day and you look as though you could use some of Alumn's blessed light." Alador turned back to Venali. "Take a scouting party and patrol the borders. I'm sure it's nothing, but further investigation will determine that."

Venali dipped his chin and left, ignoring Trey like they hadn't fucked each other raw last night. That was fine with Trey. The last thing he wanted was Venali's group of fans getting it in their heads there was anything between Trey and their fearless harem leader.

"Trouble?" Trey asked.

"No, just some unusual finds. Some of our goats have been mauled, but unusually for wolves, they've left the carcasses. Could be nothing. Venali will take care of it."

Alador led Trey out of Ashford, into the gardens, where other elves roamed, soaking up the sun. "A wonder isn't it...?" the elder said. "We live like our ancestors before us, free to do as we wish beneath Alumn's rays."

Alumn was smiling down on them this morning, shining her rays, making butterflies flit and dance. The fact that she was both dragon and elf didn't seem to have deterred anyone here from enjoying her wealth of nature and light. "It's certainly new."

"We have vast plans for Ashford. Other villages too. The humans are graciously helping us with electrics and plumbing. But the changes take some adjusting." Alador clasped his hands behind his back and lifted his face to the sun. "Eroan mentioned in his note to me that you've spent some time training Order assassins."

Trey nodded. "I did. Until it became clear we—they were no longer needed."

"I have prides of Order assassins, like you, who find themselves without a trade. When you've trained your entire life to kill, it can be difficult learning to tend potatoes."

"Yes." What else was he supposed to say? Surely Alador didn't want a solution from Trey? Didn't he have council members to talk such things over with? "Eroan has coped by... Well, by going off in search of other battles, I think." That wasn't really coping, he realized. Maybe assassins wouldn't ever cope. That was how things were with them. They each had to find their way in this new world, a world none of them were prepared for.

Alador nodded. "He always did have restless feet, that one. A little like you." The elder smiled knowingly.

"I was a messenger before joining the Order. Wandering is in my blood. More so than killing."

Alador smiled fondly. "Of course. When do you plan to move on from Ashford?"

"Tomorrow morning."

"I have some notes for Eroan. Will you see they get to him?"

"He's not likely to be back for a few months at least, but I'll see your notes are waiting."

"Good, good..." Alador walked on, content to soak up the sun. "I wonder if you might help me with a more sensitive matter. I have some concerns about my assassins, but also regarding Venali."

"Oh?" Trey hedged. This could get awkward real fast.

"This period of adjustment has hit some of our kin harder than others."

A cloud sailed over the sun, instantly chilling the air and darkening the gardens. Alador stopped on the path. His entire body stilled, turning from friendly elder into ancient assassin in the space of a blink. "I've seen a great many things in all my years and I know better than most that some of us are better equipped to deal with change than others. You're one of those who adjusts. You've seen tragedy, as have we all, but it has not eroded your light."

It had eroded something in Trey. He smiled less, laughed less, danced less, but he got by. Moving on helped. "I'm not sure what you're asking of me."

"Just that... *Some* of us need a steadying hand before we steer ourselves into darkness."

"Some do. Yes. And this has something to do with me?"

"Doesn't it?"

Trey was obviously missing something. Alador couldn't know about last night, unless Venali had told him, and that didn't seem likely given the icy reception. "Alador, what is it you think I can do for your assassins in a day? I'll be gone tomorrow."

The elder nodded. "Battles are lost and won in a day."

What battle was he referring to? "If this is somehow about Venali, he seems perfectly capable of surviving any battle thrown his way."

Alador flinched, actually flinched. There was definitely something missing here. "He does, doesn't he."

"Venali has plenty of acquaintances to fall back on. Whatever you're asking, I don't think I'm suitable."

"Of course." He smiled sadly. "I'm sorry I mentioned anything. Please enjoy the rest of your stay, Trey, and give my regards to Eroan when you see him. Perhaps he might like to visit us again soon?"

Trey nodded and let the elder walk on, just as the sun poked through the clouds again, washing the land and the shining walls of Ashford in warmth.

~

THERE WAS no dagger in his door at sunset, so perhaps the assassins weren't partying tonight, or maybe Trey wasn't invited. He decided to avoid the library and instead chose to rest for the trek ahead of him. He was due to take the north trails along the coast and visit the next settlement. It wasn't far, but the terrain was harsh. He'd need to be well rested and fed before leaving.

He slept restlessly that night and woke to a gray and rain-filled view from his window. Lacing up his traveling boots, he repacked his pack, threw on his coat, and headed for the main desk to collect his messenger bag.

A substantial crowd had gathered around the tree, watching someone high up in its branches tie a ribbon to a branch. Another colored ribbon meant another death. Adding ribbons to the tree was once a daily occurrence across the land. These days, it was much rarer.

Conor was at the desk. His mouth flirted with a smile on seeing Trey, but it didn't reach his eyes.

"What happened?" Trey asked.

Conor lifted the dispatch bag on the desk and retied the buckles. "We lost an assassin last night."

Trey looked again at the group around the tree, recognizing some of the faces from the library. Venali wasn't present, but Kalie was, her head lifted to the light, tears wet on her cheeks.

"Bandits?"

"No, she, er..." Conor handed over the bag. "She was found in her room," he said grimly. "She'd taken her blade to her wrists."

An assassin had taken her own life? The horror of such a thing sent a chill through Trey. He'd never known of an elf willingly sending themselves to Alumn's garden. Shock stole his voice.

"Safe travels, Trey," Conor nodded. "Check in when you're

next round this way?" He offered his hand and Trey clasped it hard in his own. Conor's eyes held too much of a glossy sheen.

"May Alumn's light guide you," Trey replied.

Conor squeezed his hand, let go, and busied himself behind the desk.

Trey heaved his bag onto his shoulders, whispered a prayer to Alumn, and headed out of Ashford, into the rain.

SNOW CAKED the ground when Trey next returned to Ashford. Bundled up in furs, he was well-equipped for winter, but entering Ashford's warm atrium with its glowing open fires and decorated walkways instantly lifted his spirits. The decorations were a human custom, apparently. Colored strings hung from door-to-door, marking their winter celebration. It was a testament to how far they'd come that the elves of Ashford were content to let the humans have their festival.

The female at the welcome desk didn't seem to know any Conor. After handing over his bag, Trey settled into his room, stripped out of the winter gear, showered, soaked hot water into his bones, dressed in a sweater and trousers, then set out in search of any familiar faces.

He wasn't looking for Venali and certainly hadn't been scanning the residents for any sign of the sentinel's signature red hair. Trey had had other lovers during his time away. It wasn't as though Venali had left the kind of impression that branded itself into Trey's thoughts and kept him warm during the frigid winter treks.

He wandered through Ashford and came upon the library, finding it was... a library, full of books and not Order assassins. As lovely as the books were, he'd been looking for music and company. Maybe Alador had put an end to the revelry?

Disappointment clung to him as he returned to his room. There may have been a few nights during the past few months during which he'd imagined returning to Ashford and falling back into the atmosphere at the library, catching up with Kalie and Conor. Now that the library was gone, and he was alone, he wondered why he'd bothered returning at all. There were the messages he carried, of course, but he could have waited a few more weeks until the snow thawed.

He sat on the bed and looked out the window, watching snowflakes flurry against the glass. There was a coldness inside him, too, one he tried to bury, but with every trek, it was becoming more and more difficult to ignore. He'd needed the library to still be there, needed the company it had promised. Nowhere else on all his travels had called to his soul like the library had.

He refused to believe the assassins didn't gather anywhere. They needed to be among their own, like he clearly needed it, too, if just for a little while before moving on again.

As night fell, he wandered Ashford's many linked walkways and corridors, admiring the humans' colored strings and bows. Catching sight of a pair of assassins—only Order assassins wore the long-distance glare of someone who'd spent their every breath thinking about the best way to kill—Trey followed them deeper into Ashford's older sections, where the walls closed and oil lamps fought off the dark. The music found him first, and he grinned. He followed the sound down some steps.

A guard at the doorway ahead blocked the way. "Blade?"

Trey dropped his hand to where he normally carried his sword, but he'd left it behind in his room. "I don't have it on me."

"No blade, no entry."

"I was here last year."

The guard narrowed his eyes.

"You were in the library then? Kalie... Is Kalie here? Tell her I'm Trey." The guard wasn't budging. "C'mon, I need this," he admitted.

"If you need it so bad, why haven't you been back since the library?"

"I travel. I'm a messenger."

"Then you're not of the Order." The guard moved to shut the door and shut Trey out.

Trey wedged his foot in the gap. "I was."

There was another name he could drop, but the thought of mentioning Venali had Trey's insides explicitly knotting. "Would you just go ask Kalie if she knows me?"

"Kalie isn't here," the brute grumbled.

Three more elves approached behind Trey, eyeing him warily. He stepped aside, letting them pass, and the guard did the same, clearly recognizing them. Trey got a glimpse of the crowd, the colored lights and shifting shadows, and felt his heart slip. Alumn, he needed to be in there.

"Go back and get your blade," the guard said with a sigh. "I can't let you in without one."

"You let them in."

"I know them. I don't know you."

"Look... Would you... Is Venali in there?"

The guard smiled and looked over Trey again. "You don't look his type."

"I'm not," Trey replied sharply. "He knows who I am. Is he in there?"

"If I let everyone in who says they know Venali, I'd have half of damn Ashford in here. You're not getting in without a blade, and the more you piss me off, the less likely I am to ever let you in. If you've even got a blade, which I'm starting to doubt, go get it."

He should, and it would solve this, but Trey squared up to

the guard instead. "I cut down dragons to help save Ashford and this is how you thank me?"

"A true Assassin of the Order doesn't need thanks." The guard kicked Trey's foot clear and slammed the door shut.

"Fuck!"

He should have handled it better, and now he was shut out of the only place he'd wanted to return to in months, looking like some Order reject who'd just tried to talk his way into a club he didn't belong in. And maybe he didn't belong? Most Order assassins were trained from the time they could walk. Trey had just fallen into it like he fell into everything in life.

"Shit, shit, shit..." He paced the narrow corridor.

"Having some problems?" a deep, rough voice enquired, the same voice Trey wished he didn't have to hear over and over in his dreams.

He looked up the steps and saw Venali standing at the top, looking down on him as though Trey were a bug to be squashed beneath his fine leather boots. Boots that went all the way up to his knees. He'd cut off his long locks to jaw-length, making his face seem even more severe, although, at this moment, he appeared to be half smiling, softening the tough sentinel. He'd caught Trey in need of assistance. Again.

"I don't have my blade," Trey said briskly. Venali started down the steps, alone. No entourage, not this time. Dressed to kill meant a whole new thing around him. Black trousers hugged a narrow waist and a purple shirt lay open at the cuffs and collar, advertising the kissable, golden skin beneath. Trey had wondered what he'd feel like seeing Venali again, whether his reaction the first time had been due to too much wine. But as Venali brushed past and Trey recalled exactly where he'd gripped his waist, lust spilled easily into Trey's veins all over again. Alumn, the desire hadn't faded. He still wanted Venali, and it wasn't some passing urge. The sudden flush of need made Trey swallow hard and steer his thoughts far from how Venali's trousers hugged the curves of his ass.

Venali rapped on the door. The guard opened it, straightened at the sight of Venali, and noticing Trey, he swallowed.

"He's with me," Venali said, already stepping inside.

And just like that, Trey was back inside the warmth and wonder of whatever this place was called. Bodies swayed to the music, pressed close in the subdued light. Someone nudged him in the shoulder, turning him around.

"An assassin is never without his blade," Venali whispered against Trey's ear, the implication clear. Trey wasn't assassin enough to remember his blade. The asshole just had to get a dig in. Trey turned back, expecting to find Venali close, but he'd vanished among the crowd. For an attention whore, he sure knew how to disappear.

Kalie's immediately familiar presence drew his eye. She'd graduated to pouring a number of drinks from different bottles, grinning from ear to ear at her customers. Nobody seemed to pay or trade goods for the drinks, just like before. Maybe Alador had something to do with that.

"Kalie..."

"Ah, Trey!" She planted a drink in his hand.

"At least *you* remember me."

"I could never forget a face as pretty as yours, my darling."

They caught up, spoke some more about traveling and how well she was keeping before Trey asked, "Is Conor around?"

"Conor?" Confusion briefly dislodged her smile. "Oh, Conor, sure... I mean, he doesn't come around much now. Venali and he... They have a thing."

A thing.

Right.

A thing without Trey.

That was okay. Honestly, what had he been expecting? It

had only been a quick fuck, and Trey had left them, making it clear it had meant nothing more.

"I'm sure he'd love to know you're here, though," Kalie said, raising her voice over the sound of the rowdy crowd. "Ask Venali where he is."

"Yeah, maybe no." He downed the drink in one gulp, and Kalie hastily poured him another.

She asked about messaging and any gossip from the neighboring villages. The more Trey talked and the more cups of wine he finished off, the more the weight of traveling lifted off his back and the more he felt like maybe he was coming home. If just for a little while.

The evening wore on into the dead of night, but the musicians kept right on playing and the drinks kept flowing. Trey had found himself part of a small, friendly group, and was regaling them of the time he'd tricked a dragon into an elf trap when Kalie touched a hand to his shoulder, snapping him out of the conversation.

"Can I borrow you... real quick?"

Her smile had vanished and her laughing eyes had sobered. Something was wrong.

"Sure." He set his drink down. "What's going on?"

"I just need you to come with me." She took his hand and wove through the crowd, through a back door, and into a shadowy corridor. "Alador can't know." And with that, she shoved open a door and pulled Trey inside a small, dimly lit room. One filthy lamp spluttered. The air was tinged with something sweet and potent. Discarded bottles lay about the floor. And an unconscious male lay sprawled in the chair.

Venali.

"Is he..." *All right? Sick? Dead?*

Kalie pulled on Venali's arm, trying to shift his weight forward. The sentinel's head lolled. "C'mon, you big, pretty bastard, time to go..."

Venali's lips moved. He managed to lift a hand and appeared to stroke at Kalie's cheek, but then the hand flopped back down again.

"That's enough of that," she gently scolded. "I brought a friend." She glowered and jerked her chin at Trey. "We're going to get you back to your place." She lowered her voice, "Don't just stand there staring, help me."

It took Trey a moment to register the last words were meant for him. He scooped Venali's other arm around his shoulders and helped heave the sentinel out of the chair.

"Not through the club. Out the door, turn left and left again. There are some stairs. I'll show you the way from there."

Venali, with his long limbs and unhelpful dead weight, took some shifting and balancing to get up the stairs and along the dark corridor to his room. Trey propped him against the wall outside his room, ignoring his murmuring, while Kalie dug inside his pocket for a key. "I can't find it."

Voices traveled up the corridor.

"Shit, someone's coming... He can't be seen like this."

Trey plastered himself to Venali, grabbed his hair, held him up, and kissed him with enough passion behind it to keep others glancing away. Venali tasted like wine and something else, something sharper with a sweet kick.

"Hm..." Venali moaned, chasing the kiss as Trey pulled back, but his eyes were unfocused, his mind in some far-away drunken place.

"You owe me, both of you. Hold him." Trey handed Venali's slumped weight over to Kalie and kicked the lock, popping the door open.

Trey grabbed an arm, and together with Kalie, managed to half carry, half drag Venali into the bedroom. "Why am I here and not Conor?"

"Conor and him... it's complicated."

Of course it fucking was.

Trey eased Venali onto the bed, making sure to prop his head up should he vomit any of the copious amounts of alcohol he'd clearly been drinking.

"I gotta get back..." Kalie headed out the bedroom door.

"You can't leave him alone like this." Trey followed her out of the room.

"He's not alone. He's got you."

"Me?" Shit, the last thing he wanted to be doing was babysitting an unconscious Venali. "And if Conor shows up?"

"Great." She grinned. "But he won't. I'll come by in the morning." She pulled the door closed behind her. Some part of it fell off and clanged to the floor.

Trey planted both hands on his hips and sighed at the empty living area. Why him? Why not one of Venali's other friends, someone who actually cared?

Returning to the bedroom, Trey lingered in the doorway.

Venali lay sprawled on his back, one arm thrown off the bed, his chest rising and falling steadily. Asleep, and without the snarling, he almost looked like someone Trey wouldn't mind spending more time with. Still impossibly imposing, even passed out cold.

Dragging a chair to the bed, Trey dumped himself into it and glowered. Venali still wore the gloves. Always with the gloves. He was tempted to sneak a look beneath them, but unlike Venali, he wasn't a prick.

Two nights he had in Ashford, and this was how he got to spend his first, staring at Venali's unconscious body.

Trey dropped his head back, "Alumn, save me from the damaged ones."

TREY WOKE stiff from hours propped in a chair and not

nearly hungover enough. The bed was empty. His heart tripped, thoughts careening off into the worst-case scenario that saw Venali dead on the floor somewhere, until he heard water running in a side room. Probably a shower.

Finally, he could leave.

Stretching, he winced around the aches and returned to the ridiculously large living area. He'd been right the first time, the view of the meadow through all the windows was stunning.

"Tea?"

Trey jumped and frowned. Venali had padded in barefoot, his body clad in loose cotton pants and a buttonless shirt. His wet hair was ruffled and messy about his face. He showed no signs of being too wasted to drag his ass home, and in fact, looked as fresh as spring morning. The way his clothing hugged all the right places, he clearly wasn't wearing underwear. Not that Trey cared, or was looking.

"I need to get cleaned up," Trey ground out, sounding like he was the one who'd had the rough night.

"Use my shower."

It wasn't a question. Trey's instincts bristled. He and Kalie had carried Sentinel Venali home and made it so nobody knew he was a washed-up mess of an assassin, and Trey didn't even get a glance, a thank-you, or even a smile. In fact, he was too busy making his own tea to even look up.

The gloves were missing.

As Trey moved closer to the cupboards and countertops where Venali was focused on his hot water and tea, he watched the male's pale hands move, seeing the unmistakable ripple of burned skin stretched tight over the backs of both hands. Dragonfire had scarred him, there was no mistaking it.

Venali reached above his head and took a second cup from the cupboard, then poured hot water over a tea strainer, clearly choosing to ignore Trey's protests.

"Maybe I will take you up on that shower..."

Venali didn't respond. He reminded Trey of a cat his ma had had when Trey had been very small. The damn thing ignored him day and night unless it wanted something. Then it had vanished one day and never came back and nobody cared but Trey.

He showered quickly, using Venali's lemony soap, dried off, and emerged to find a pile of folded clothes waiting for him. Wearing Venali's clothes seemed like a step too far. Trey dressed in his own clothes from last night and returned to the living area to find Venali at the window, drinking his tea. His hair had dried, turning wavy, inviting Trey's fingers to run through it. That thought caught Trey off guard and set his feet in motion again. He picked up his tea, wrapped his fingers around the hot mug, and took a sip. Honey and lemon, with a hint of ginger root. It was good and hit the empty spot leftover from last night's lack of sleep.

"Thank you," Venali said.

Trey blinked, leaned against the counter, and admired the sun-draped enigma that was Venali. "You're welcome."

The quiet rolled on, indicating no further explanation was coming, and Trey supposed he wasn't exactly entitled to one. It wasn't as though they were friends.

The door dumped open, squeaking on its bent hinges. "Good, you're up. Hey, Trey." Kalie strode in, heading straight for Venali.

"Hey." Trey took another sip and watched her over the rim of the mug.

"Venali, you're lucky we weren't seen. Alador—"

"Doesn't need to know."

She stopped a few strides behind him. "You gotta sort your shit out. If Trey hadn't been there, Alador would know by now, and..."

"And what?" Venali turned.

"I know what it feels like," she sighed. "We all know. If it happens again, I'm going to have to tell him."

Venali's sharp laugh held no humor. "You really don't."

"You're supposed to be our sentinel. Fuck, we're supposed to look up to you. I can't keep scraping your ass off the floor. I can't watch you do this to yourself."

Venali's cheek fluttered. He looked down. "I'm fine."

"Fine?" She laughed and threw a pleading look at Trey. "None of us are fine. We lost Shannon last night."

Venali's head snapped up. "How?"

"Same as the others."

Okay, this was different. Both of their stances had hardened, shutting down or shutting off. Trey set his tea aside.

"Alador knows?" Venali asked, approaching Kalie.

"Of course."

"Shit, Kalie..." He reached for her, but she jerked back.

"You're supposed to be on this, Venali!"

"I am—"

"You're not."

Anger flared in the male's eyes. "Short of watching every Order assassin every night, what would you have me do?" he demanded, voice raised.

"Something! Anything. Besides passing out while good people kill themselves."

Trey stilled, gripping the edge of the counter. The quiet ticked on, the words falling hard.

"This is not my doing, Kalie." Venali's jaw hardened. "I am not responsible for every Order life. I'm barely responsible for my own."

"I know." She sighed. "I know, I just... I knew Shannon. I saw her almost every night. We trained together." She sniffed and threw her shoulders back. "It was more than that. We aren't supposed to have relationships. We knew that, but... Venali... Why?!"

Venali swooped in and bundled her in his arms, murmuring words Trey didn't catch. She sobbed against him, and Trey's heart felt that pain too. Assassins weren't supposed to die now. But clearly, they continued to.

He bowed his head, looking away from the private moment, giving them space.

"I'm sorry about last night, " Kalie said. She'd pulled from Venali's arms and wiped her face. "Thank you, Trey."

"It's fine. You have enough to worry over."

She smiled warmly. "I knew you were one of the good ones." She left without saying another word.

Venali stared at the broken door. He waited a few quiet moments before saying, "Two nights and you get to walk away." He retreated to the bedroom, leaving Trey alone.

"Sometimes walking away is harder than it looks," Trey mumbled softly. He was beginning to understand why Venali was like he was. They were all damaged, some in more ways than others, and Venali was damaged in a way that went deeper than the scars on his hands. Trey had seen it before. Alumn, he lived with the memories every day. And now, with the self-inflicted deaths, it seemed as though living with the hurt had become too much for some.

TREY LEFT the tea and Venali and returned to his own room to catch up on the sleep he'd lost watching the sentinel. He'd be back on the road soon and a bed was a luxury he planned to enjoy while he could.

Knuckles rapped on his door. Groaning, he buried his head under the pillow and waited for whomever it was to go away. The knocks came again, more insistent this time.

"All right!" he called. Scraping himself off the bed, he

ruffled his hair, threw on a shirt and pants, and opened the door.

Sentinel Venali stood in the hallway, wrapped in his work clothes, just missing his bow and quiver of red-fletched arrows. His eyes widened briefly before he shut down the slip in his mask.

"Come with me."

Alumn, he said it like Trey was in some kind of trouble. Of course, the authoritative tone coupled with Venali's gravelly voice woke other parts of Trey.

"You're asking or telling?" Trey grumbled, folding his arms.

"Asking."

"Didn't sound like it."

Venali's lips pinched. "Would you please assist me with a sensitive matter, Trey?"

"Of course, Venali. Give me a few moments and I'll be right out." He closed the door in Venali's face and bumped his forehead against it.

"Bring your blade," Venali said, voice muffled from behind the door.

"Will I be needing it?" Trey called back.

"I need you as an Order assassin, not a messenger."

You need me? Trey squeezed his eye closed. Okay, so he hadn't stopped thinking about Venali in months. Really, the male was exactly why Trey was here early, but now that he had Venali's attention, he wasn't entirely sure what to do with it. Last night, seeing him wrecked and vulnerable, Alumn, it had flicked on Trey's instincts to protect, and now he couldn't seem to shake it. Venali did not need protection. Anyway, this was clearly business.

Trey retrieved his blade, hooking it onto his belt, shrugged on a loose coat, ran his fingers through his hair, maybe checked his appearance in the mirror a few times, and finally met Venali outside.

"What do you need me for?"

Wild, raw sex, my room, right now, Trey imagined.

Venali walked ahead. "Shannon, the Order assassin who took her own life. I want you to visit her room with me. Are you going to be all right with this?"

Trey's budding lust fizzled to nothing. He'd seen more dead bodies than he'd ever wanted to. He was never okay with it. "Is her body still there?"

"No, but there is blood." Venali marched on, voice matter-of-fact.

"It's fine."

They walked on, passing down stairs and along an open landing lined with residential rooms. "Alador said Eroan trained you to recruit and train your own pride of assassins."

"Nye trained me. Eroan had me in a role to recruit and train further assassins."

"Nye?" The way he'd asked suggested he'd heard of Nye. Whatever he'd heard, it probably wasn't good. "He was a formidable assassin... before the end."

Nye had been a fucking mess. Trey had tried to save Nye from Nye, but it had been too little too late. By the time Trey really knew him, Nye was already too lost in his own head to accept help. In the end, his ambitions, desires, whatever they were, had killed him.

Trey cleared the sudden knot in his throat. "He was."

Venali approached a door on the ground level, heavily guarded by two Order assassins, bristling with weapons. They dipped their chins at Venali and opened the door.

The smell of blood, one not forgotten easily, burned Trey's nose and laced his throat. Dark stains had soaked into the rugs, the floor, and bed, where the female must have lain to perform her final desperate act. Her body wasn't there, as

Venali had said, but her outline indented the sheets. And that almost felt worse. She'd been there, and now she was gone. Forever.

"There's a lot of blood," Trey remarked, needing to speak. He sounded hoarse.

"The humans have a word for it when one of their kind takes their own life. They call it suicide."

Trey wanted to ask why he'd been brought here. What was he supposed to say or do? What, by Alumn, did Venali expect from him?

"Elves don't have a word for this," Venali continued. He drifted about the room, carefully appraising the upset sheets and stains.

"Because we don't do this."

No elf would take their own life. It was unheard of. Even among damaged and abandoned assassins. Until now. "How many have done this?"

"Three."

"Three?!" That seemed like a lot. "Since when?"

"Since you were last here."

"What's triggering it?" Trey asked, approaching the heavily stained side of the bed and crouching down to eye the rug's hardened fibers.

"What do you mean?" Venali asked.

"What's changed? Why now? Why haven't we seen this before?"

The sentinel considered the question with a frown. "Nothing."

"Are they connected?" Trey asked.

"They're assassins."

Trey looked up. "Does anything else connect them? Did they know each other? Were they close? Maybe they'd made some kind of agreement to do this... *suicide* together?"

"No, no connection, other than they were all part of the

After Dark club..." Venali glanced at the door. "But all assassins are."

So, that's what the Order gathering place was called. Trey arched an eyebrow and straightened. "I've seen wounds bleed out, arteries cut..." He gestured at the bed, the spray marks, and the floor. "This is messy. Like she panicked."

"Assassins don't panic."

"They might when taking their own life." He skipped his attention around the rest of the room and saw the Order blade on the bloody dresser. "Is that what she used?"

"We believe so." Venali reached for the blade, then stopped and withdrew his gloved fingers. He looked again at the bed, the blade, and the door.

"What is it?"

Typically ignoring Trey, Venali went to the door and asked one of the guards something. Trey heard the murmuring but couldn't make out the words. Whatever the answer was, it had hardened Venali's face. "Have you seen enough?" he asked Trey.

"I don't really know what you expected me to see."

"Follow me." To the guards, Venali added, "Nobody gets inside this room without my permission."

Trey strode alongside Venali, breathing hard to match his pace. Clearly, something about the scene bothered him, something to do with the blade. But the sentinel wouldn't be pushed for answers.

"Sometimes, we love our own kind so much we hesitate to see the truth," Venali said suddenly.

Trey clenched his jaw, feeling the words too close to his heart to answer without revealing the hurt they'd summoned. He hadn't properly thought of Nye in weeks, but Venali's words tore Trey's shields wide open and let the memories tumble in. Nye had been his teacher, and Alumn, Trey had fallen for the fragile moments he'd seen in him. The shy smiles and soft caresses. Nye could have been saved, if only Trey had known how.

Venali glanced over, his green eyes shrewd. "Shannon didn't take her own life. She was killed."

To think such a thing was almost worse than elves considering suicide. "Are you sure?" Trey asked, speaking under his breath.

"No, and I fear I may be grasping at a better reason for all this, but there is much wrong with that room. The blood, the way in which it spread, she either panicked—as you said—or she fought. And now, I find myself going over my memory of the previous deaths. This isn't right. It doesn't feel right." He stared ahead, anger rolling off him in waves. "The guards found the blade on the dresser, where we saw it, not in her hand. Someone left it there."

If Venali was right, someone was killing Order assassins.

VENALI PULLED Alador from his council meeting. The elder acknowledged Trey with a nod and a smile, but the smile soon vanished as Venali explained his theory. Alador instructed Venali to investigate the previous scenes again, despite the locations having been cleaned months ago.

Trey assisted, where he could, watching Venali methodically go back over the locations of the previous deaths, but there was nothing of use to be found.

The more Venali threw himself into the task, the more Trey caught himself quietly observing the male, watching him as he spoke with anyone who might have seen the *victims* before their deaths. He was careful not to call them victims and asked their surviving kin with reverence and respect.

Kalie had been right. He really was a very different person when working. In the coat with its Ashford symbol, he became someone others clearly looked up to. He even reminded Trey a little of Eroan, which was no easy feat.

Dusk crept upon them again. Trey was due to leave for another trek tomorrow, but he wasn't ready to think on it yet.

Venali led them back to his room. The door had been fixed from where Trey had kicked it in earlier that morning. Venali straightened. He looked at the spot beside the door for a few moments. There was no way Venali remembered the kiss. Was there?

"Will you be at AD tonight?" Venali asked, the question, like his eyes, as penetrating as always.

Dragons couldn't tear Trey away. But he wasn't about to admit it. "I leave tomorrow so... I should really get some sleep. Winter is a bitch on the bones."

"Right, because you're only here for two nights..." Venali opened the door, but lingered outside, looking curiously awkward as he hesitated. "Today was... Thank you. For helping me."

"You're welcome. I'm sorry we didn't find anything of use."

"I'd like to see you tonight at AD."

Well, hello there, broody and vulnerable. Trey schooled his features and was glad Venali couldn't hear his leaping heart. "All right."

"Bring your blade." His smart mouth ticked at the corners.

"I'll do that."

Venali entered his room, and Trey left before having to say anything awkward like *goodbye* or *see you later*.

Shit, they'd mostly had a real, normal conversation. Was tonight a date? Was that what just happened? Had Venali asked him out? Trey would take it. Because tomorrow, he'd be gone again, and life was too short for regrets.

TREY SHOWED the guard his blade and grinned.

The male rolled his eyes and grumbled, "Yeah, yeah. Come on in."

The band was different, this one with a young, female singer who tapped out a beat on her thigh along with the rest of her musicians. The crowd had thinned some, too, but it was still early.

Kalie waved him over. "Come back here and help me line up these clean cups, will you?"

He happily obliged, setting to work on lining up the cups from a stack of crates. "Where does the wine come from?"

"The local village grape crop mostly. They bottle it in late autumn and store it for the next year. We get shipments free, because, you know... we're who we are."

"Trey." Conor grinned, planting himself against the bar. "I heard you were back." He offered his hand and Trey gripped it fondly, beaming back.

"I missed you at the desk."

"Ah, yeah... I don't work there anymore. I work the fields now." Trey waited for more of an explanation, but Conor looked around, probably searching for Venali, before settling his attention back on Trey again. "I didn't expect to see you again until the new year. How long are you in for?"

Trey picked up a corked bottle, popped the cork, and poured Conor a drink, then poured himself one. "I leave tomorrow."

"Tomorrow, huh?" He smiled shyly. "Are you busy here right now?"

Kalie took the bottle from Trey's hand. "No, he's not. You boys go catch up."

"I'll be right out," Trey stalled.

"Sure." Conor drifted off.

Trey caught Kalie's raised eyebrow. "I really need to know what the deal is between him and Venali," he asked, on the quiet.

"On and off again. They've been like that a while now. I was surprised to see Conor with you the last time you were here, actually. He knows how Venali feels... I mean, he, er... Shit." She swallowed any further words behind a gulp of drink.

"Wait. What?"

"What?"

"You were saying... something about Venali?"

"Oh Alumn. Look. Venali... may have mentioned you a few times since the battle. Asking after you, that kind of thing."

"What? Why?"

She huffed. "Don't be dense."

"He hardly knows me."

"Exactly. Forget I said anything. Nothing to see here. Move along."

A line of customers chose that moment to swarm Kalie's bar. She nudged Trey out with a wink and deliberately busied herself. She was not getting away with that so easily. He'd be back later and made sure she saw it on his face.

She looked over, checking he was leaving, and he pointed back at her, mouthing, *"Not finished with you,"* making her grin.

Trey knew the moment Venali arrived. The atmosphere shifted and a line of tension strummed the crowd. It was respect and more. For Venali, it must have felt as though the world rested on his shoulders, but he didn't show it. He had someone with him. A new face, a female folded in the crook of his arm. The music was too loud to hear what she said, but whatever it was, it had Venali grinning like he hadn't spent the entire day revisiting the rooms of dead Order elves.

Conor slipped an arm through Trey's and drew him aside

to an empty table with cushioned benches. He produced a bottle and placed it between them. "So we only have tonight before you're gone again?"

From his grin, he was clearly thinking on what came after the wine. Trey wasn't about to say no, but Kalie's comment niggled at the back of his thoughts. Trey had assumed he'd been the one to pick Conor up the last time, but maybe Conor had singled him out because of *something* to do with Venali. The pair clearly had a relationship. "Listen, Conor... I don't want to get between you and Venali."

"There isn't anything between me and Venali." He laughed easily. "I mean, look at him..."

Trey stole a glance, only to find Venali tucked in tightly with the female in one arm and an older male in the other. Trey had a good idea where that threesome was heading later and was surprised to feel a twinge of jealousy. Venali had invited him here, but why? So Trey could watch him get off with another pair?

Conor leaned back, smiling coyly. "What the three of us had last time, though, I'd be game for *that* again."

Trey glanced again, watching Venali's long, gloved fingers stroke over the male's thigh. "He looks pretty occupied already." He'd been hoping he might have experienced that smooth tease from those gloved fingers, especially as how they'd left things earlier in the evening, but now Venali clearly had his sights set on someone else.

Shit, Trey had known he was like this, but after spending the day with him, and after helping scoop him off the floor last night, he'd thought there had been a little more between them than a passing fuck. Frankly, just another threesome would be enough, especially as Trey clearly wasn't needed for anything else.

"Don't look so down. He hasn't seen you yet," Conor said.

"I don't think he cares whether I'm here or not."

Conor's brow pinched. "You don't know?"

"Know what? I feel like I'm missing something."

"Go to the bar," Conor grinned, "talk with Kalie. He'll see you. I bet he comes right on over like he did before."

Considering Venali's wandering hands, it didn't look like much short of a dragon would distract him. But it was worth testing. Especially as this was Trey's final night, and if he left without tasting Venali again, he'd never get any sleep on the road.

"I bet you an earring he sees me and doesn't care," Trey said, adding a half smile. Better to make light of all this than show any sign of whatever this mess was in his head.

Conor grinned. "You're on."

"You're losing an earring."

Conor crossed his arms, looking mighty confident. "Sure I am..."

Kalie arched an eyebrow as Trey approached her bar. He already had a drink in his hand. "You have a hungry look in your dark eyes, messenger," she purred.

"Just go with it." He leaned against the bar and checked on Venali across the bar behind her, catching the precise moment Venali looked over. Shit, Trey didn't believe in all that first sight bullshit, but Venali's sudden, unblinking eyes locking on him delivered a breathless jolt of lust, making him reveal way too much with a gasp.

He tried to hide it by taking a drink, but Kalie heard, checked to see who he was looking at, and chuckled. "Would you two fuck already?"

Trey felt his lips reveal too much of a smile. "Venali's not my type."

Kalie flicked a hand. "Who says you have to like him to fuck him?"

"Kalie," Trey acted shocked, "you are full of surprises."

Venali was currently extracting himself from the clinging

limbs of his companions. He *was* coming over, and Trey's wretched heart did a little fluttering skip. The anticipation alone was getting him hard, again in public. By Alumn, Venali was something else and he was heading right over, just like Conor had predicted. Did that mean something?

"Venali!" Kalie beamed. "Well, don't you look mighty fine tonight? Better than when Trey and I peeled your ass off the floor."

Venali leaned against the bar, caught Kalie's chin with his gloved fingers, and leaned in, placing a delicate kiss on her forehead. "What would I do without you?"

"Drink yourself into Alumn's garden?" She playfully batted his hand away. "Get out of here. The three of you making eyes at each is distracting as hell."

Venali turned his head, looking behind him. Conor raised his cup, wearing a lopsided grin. Venali faced Trey, making Trey's skin simmer. They all knew what they wanted, but getting there required small talk nobody wanted. "That room from last night... The one out back..." Trey began, letting the sentence hang, possibilities lingering in the unspoken.

Venali pushed off the bar and headed for Conor, leaving Trey to assume he was following. Kalie waggled her eyebrows and blew him a kiss, waving him away. He drifted after Venali, watching the sentinel offer Conor his hand and gracefully lift him to his feet. Heat touched Conor's cheeks. He melted around Venali, likely even loved him, but if he wanted to share, which clearly he did, Trey would play the third wheel. He couldn't expect any more, not with a messenger's life.

Any evidence of Venali's episode had been cleaned away from the room. A couch and a chair, no windows, nothing fancy, just the one door in and out. Venali entered first, fingers already unlacing his waistcoat. Conor lit the single lamp, chasing the dark into the corners, and then turned the flame down, making the shadows slide across the walls.

Trey's heart beat in his throat, making him breathless. He closed the door behind them. He was already hard and acutely aware of both males. Venali's long fingers laid his waistcoat gently on the back of the couch, his every motion precise and elegant. Artful. Elegance was the last thing from Trey's mind. Patience was pretty far off too. There was pleasure to be had in the wait, but Alumn, it was killing him to hold back and pretend nonchalance.

Conor pulled off his shirt, and as Venali turned to face him, Conor kissed him, long and slow, mouth open, tongue gently probing. Venali had his hand in his hair, holding Conor firm, but his gaze flicked to Trey and burned, making Trey's cock jump. Venali's attention roamed downward, finding his target eagerly pushing against the inside of Trey's trousers. Venali undressed Trey with his eyes, and it was all Trey could do to stand still and let it happen. Then Conor broke the kiss, switching to Venali's neck. Unbuttoning Venali's shirt, Conor roamed his kisses down Venali's warm, hard chest.

The last time they'd done this, Trey had pleasured Venali from behind. He hadn't needed to look the sentinel in the eyes. Now, Venali's intense glare had skewed him to the spot as Venali guided Conor's head downward. On his knees, Conor worked on Venali's trouser ties, yanking them open. He grasped his prize and licked from balls to tip.

Venali's lips parted, his eyes bright with color, pupils blown wide.

Trey was done observing. He pulled his sweater off, leaving his snug undershirt on. Venali could remove it if he wanted more.

Conor closed his mouth over Venali's taut cock, making Venali's lashes flutter closed. Trey caught Venali's jaw and turned his head away. He wanted Venali's mouth on him, but not yet. There would be time for that. Right now, he needed to exert control. Trey kissed his neck and slipped a hand around Venali's waist, relishing the hard warmth of lean muscle shuddering at his touch.

Venali's breaths came fast, Conor working his erection as Trey swirled his tongue over his neck and down his shoulder, nipping here and there, pinching enough to make Venali gasp. Venali found Trey's pant ties and yanked, jerking Trey's crotch against Venali's hip. Sensation blurred, Trey's thoughts lost to the feel of Venali cupping Trey's arousal through the trousers. He groped hard, lifting Trey's balls, hinting at where this would go. Venali's fingers worked, loosening off the pant ties and freeing Trey's cock. Gloved fingers immediately closed over Trey's swollen rod, squeezing over the tip, triggering Trey to buck.

"Ah, fuck—"

Venali's hot mouth captured his. Trey had planned to pleasure him first, but Venali clearly had his own ideas. He kissed like he played, fast and hard, thrusting in and devouring.

Venali's hand abandoned Trey's cock, making him groan the loss into Venali's mouth, and then Conor's warm, tight, wet mouth closed over Trey's tip.

Trey gasped from Venali's mouth and looked down to where Venali's hand guided Conor's pace, while Conor's mouth worked Trey's cock. Venali controlling Conor while Conor got Trey off had to be the hottest damn thing Trey had seen in years.

"You like that?" Venali purred.

Conor took him deep, gagging slightly as Trey more than filled him. The male's lips slid down his shaft. *Yes* wasn't a strong enough word. He was losing his mind to pleasure, falling into the feel of Conor's wet, tight lips working his cock while Venali's mouth owned his neck and mouth and lips in other ways.

Gloved fingers stroked down Trey's neck tattoos, and then

Venali's mouth was on them too, his tongue a wet, probing tease.

Conor pulled free, leaving Trey's cock jumping, aching for tightness to envelop him again.

Venali eased off and pulled Conor to his feet, guiding him to the couch, where Venali knelt on one side, and then guided Conor onto the middle cushions. The male went down on him again, so willing and eager.

Trey grasped his own erection, stroking it, then wished he hadn't as pleasure shuddered tightly through him. Too much of that and he wouldn't last.

Venali tipped his head, gesturing at the side table with its single drawer. Trey found a convenient bottle of oil inside. After lathering himself up, he climbed onto the other end of the couch and took Conor's ass in his hands, stroking over his hole. With Conor placed between them, Trey couldn't look away from the stunning sight of Venali with his cock in Conor's mouth.

Trey licked down Conor's salty back and reached around the male's waist, clutching his erection. The oil made his grip loose and free. Trey circled his fingers and thumb, making a tight O, and pumped Conor's rod. Conor gasped around Venali's erection and Venali chuckled a filthy laugh.

His laughter was a wicked delight, making Trey's lips quirk.

Trey kissed Conor's back, checking every few breaths that Venali still soaked up the sight. Conor's body strummed, his hips finding their pace, thrusting through Trey's hand. He came, pulling free of Venali, spilling his seed in spurts over the couch.

While Conor shuddered out his released, Trey slid his oil-slicked cock into Conor's tight hole and nearly fucking lost his load before he'd even begun. Venali's studious observation dialed everything up to a mind-numbing intensity there was no escape from, and then Venali was rocking, fucking Conor's mouth again, his eyes locked on Trey's. Trey pumped into Conor's hot sheath. Conor's clenched passage sucked him off. Trey grunted out his pleasure.

Venali was fucking mesmerizing, his mouth open, teeth biting into his lip, his hands holding Conor beneath him, cock plunging deep.

There was no holding back, no control. Trey lost all measure of sanity, and when Venali threw his head back, shuddering his seed down Conor's throat, Trey came undone too, thrusting hard, grunting like a fucking animal, needing it faster, harder, until the pleasure snapped and the pulses pumped his seed deep into Conor's ass. He swore, gasping out the words, and shuddered from after-pulses. Alumn, he wasn't sure he'd ever come harder.

Pulling free twisted pleasure to pain. Seed dribbled from Conor's hole. Trey collected his cream on his fingertips and gently stroked around Conor's sensitive hole, making the male purr.

The burning look in Venali's eyes said this was far from over.

They dressed, exchanging short, sharp, intent-filled glances, and left the room, weaving through the crowd and out, up the stairs, needing few words to know exactly where Venali was leading them next.

Inside his home, Venali carelessly discarded his waistcoat over the back of a chair, picked up a convenient bottle of his strong mixture, and drank without missing a stride. He tore off his shirt and turned, grinned, and crooked a finger at Trey.

Trey remembered going to him, remembered making it to the bed, remembered Venali pouring the potent mix over his tongue, dribbling it down Trey's chest, then Venali lapping it up. Conor was somewhere in the midst of it all too. His grip rougher than Venali's gloved fingers, but his mouth was softer, more giving, less taking. Venali fucking owned Trey, thrusting his fingers in while his mouth took him too. There wasn't much room for thought, just touch and taste, hard muscle and shimmering skin. Once the bed was knotted and drenched, Venali had them move to the shower and started all over again, fucking and probing every hand, hole, and mouth like it was Trey's last night alive. Alumn, it was raw and hard and rough, and Trey couldn't get enough of Venali in him to satisfy his rampant lust.

After they were spent and sore and fallen atop one another, Trey dozed, knowing two nights would never be enough.

~

TREY WOKE SLOWLY, blinking into the harsh winter sunlight pouring in through Venali's bedroom windows. Rays of sunlight draped over Venali's longbow resting against the wall. The weapon was almost as tall as its owner, its curves just as desirable. A formidable weapon, like the male himself.

Warmth radiated beside Trey. He turned toward him and groaned around his body's soreness, but it was a good soreness, the kind he'd be feeling for days.

Venali lay on his back, mouth quirked in a smile, naked body spread like a buffet for Trey's enjoyment. His eyes were closed, but his half smile said he was very much awake.

Rolling onto his side, Trey stroked his fingertips down Venali's chest, scraping his nails lower, skirting the male's erection lying against his lower stomach, making Venali's smile twitch. His cock twitched, too, and Trey's mouth watered. He'd tasted all of him last night and was still fuzzy enough from the wine to want to mount Venali in the sunlight and make him cry out again. They were both clean from the shower, going another round was definitely an option. He'd lick him from cock to balls to ass. But if he did that, he'd want to stay, and the sun was already high enough.

Trey hooked a leg over Venali's thigh and flicked his tongue over his nipple.

Venali's eyes fluttered open, piercing through Trey.

He could go another round. Several, in fact. Spend the whole day wrapped in Venali. Though, they were missing their third. "Where's Conor?" Trey croaked, almost ashamed he hadn't noticed his absence sooner.

"Left at dawn," Venali grumbled, his voice wrecked. "Goats or something..."

He sounded washed-up but deliciously sated, and in his sleepy, post-sex-and-alcohol state, he looked good enough to eat. His hair was a mess, sticking out at odd angles, and his smile was the softest Trey had ever seen on his lips. Trey's heart did that strange little hiccup. He rolled onto Venali, trapping Venali's hips under his thighs, making Venali's alert cock ride up the valley of Trey's ass.

Venali's expectant expression did nothing to ease Trey's arousal, propped up between them. Trey leaned down and kissed him slowly, savoring the male he'd trapped.

Venali stroked a finger up Trey's spine, making him moan, turning the kiss messy and hungry and all the things they didn't have time for.

"Stay," Venali whispered, his chest rising and falling too fast. His fingers tangled in Trey's hair. Not gloved, Trey noticed, watching Venali twirl a lock of hair. "One more night?" His green eyes skipped away from Trey's scrutiny.

Someone like Venali didn't ask for company, it was freely thrown at his feet. What did it mean that he'd asked Trey?

Trey's skipping breaths and heart answered for him. "One more night," he agreed against the corner of Venali's mouth, then probed his tongue around its curve, luring Venali's thoughts back into the moment.

Venali's bare fingers stroked down Trey's cheek, his smile shifting, and then traveled over the tattoos and down Trey's neck. The touch felt divine and impossibly soft from someone as hard as Venali appeared to be on the outside.

"I can't feel anything..." he admitted. "I can see from your expression that it's good. I know you like it, but I can't feel you beneath my hands."

Trey stilled, but Venali continued to stroke over his shoulder and skim across his collarbone, circling and teasing his burned fingers across Trey's skin in all the right ways.

"I pulled a friend from the flames." Venali swallowed with an audible click. "He died anyway." He dropped his hand, and his guard, too, letting Trey see the hurt in his eyes. He still wore a smile, but it was a battered, broken thing. The *friend* meant more to him than just-friends usually do. "These are my marks." He turned his hand over in the sunlight, admiring how the light rippled over a patchwork of mottled scars.

"Does it hurt?"

"They ache sometimes. But I miss touch the most."

Trey settled against Venali's side and propped his head on his hand, looking down at the riddle of a male who seemed impossibly strong in the day, but so thoroughly vulnerable at night... and now. He felt things deeply, this stone-cold sentinel. More than he revealed in public.

"You mark yourself when you lose someone close." Venali's soft lashes fluttered, his eyes drinking Trey in. "Who did you lose?"

Trey touched the new tattoos on his neck. The memories all came back at once. The passion, moments stolen, and then how it all turned to darkness. Nye's mind had been too far gone to save, but that hadn't stopped Trey from trying. He dropped his hand. "A friend, like yours."

"He meant a great deal to you?"

"He did, but he... I couldn't save him either."

"I'm sorry."

"So am I."

Hearing those words briefly choked him. Trey looked down, feeling the hurt keenly. He hadn't allowed himself to hurt, not really. There had been assassins to train, and then messages to deliver, and he'd kept moving on. One foot in front of the other, time and time again. He'd failed Nye. He could have saved him, could have found a way...

"The war was never meant to end," Venali whispered, blinking at the ceiling. "Alador tells us we must live our lives, tells us to make a pride of our own, to look to a future we were never supposed to have. He tells us to change who we are. I tell the assassins the same, but it's a lie."

"Why?"

Venali turned his head, facing Trey, and for the first time, Trey saw the real Venali, the male beneath the mask. His eyes shimmered, drowned in emotion, and his mouth tilted like he tried to dam everything inside. "How can I tell them to look to the future when I cannot see tomorrow?"

Alumn, he hurt, too. All the bluster and ego, it was an act, one he wore every night for everyone else, so they saw it was possible to survive, to keep moving forward, but inside, Venali was lost.

Venali blinked quickly, catching himself before he fell. He frowned, maybe at himself, maybe at Trey, and sat up, turning away.

Trey wanted to pull him back down, to kiss him and fuck him until they both forgot the hurt, like last night, like before. Instead, he watched Venali collect his fresh clothes and dress in the work colors stamped with the Ashford tree symbol. The symbol was his shield, keeping others out. There were no more monsters to fight, not outside. But the monsters still lingered, only now they were inside.

"Don't you ever get a day off?" Trey asked, stretching beneath the sheet, hoping to lure Venali back to bed.

"Elves are dying. Nobody else is going to find out why."

And now he was right back to being the untouchable Sentinel Venali. Pillar of Ashford.

Venali pulled on his gloves, completing the picture.

"I want to help. I have one more day…"

Venali opened his mouth to protest, like he would have done in the past, but he paused, considered it, straightened his long coat, and nodded, tacking on a new, fragile smile, one that hooked into Trey's heart.

THERE SEEMED little to base Venali's murder theory on besides a hunch. If someone was killing assassins, that someone either had to be incredibly strong or well known to the victims. Assassins didn't die easily.

Having a killer among them didn't seem likely, but neither did suicide. Perhaps a dragonkin had snuck in among the humans, but dragons could be sniffed out. Any dragonkin wouldn't have been able to hide in Ashford for long. That left human or elf.

After a second day of questioning, they'd failed to uncover any new information. This time, when dusk came around and Venali finished his work, he invited Trey inside his mind with no more than a flick of his hand.

Trey made the tea while Venali stripped out of his uniform and reappeared dressed to kill, yet again. There were other elves in Ashford who enjoyed similar luxuries; it wasn't just Venali. But he made everyone else look like wild, ragged elflings scrabbling in the dirt.

"Who makes your clothes?" Trey fought off a laugh.

Venali folded his arms beside Trey and leaned a hip against the counter, looking like some perfect picture of sophisticated elf that Trey wanted to rip open with his teeth and dry fuck into a wall. "I can introduce you to her if you like? Alumn knows you could do with a little style. Yours is a little... *wild*."

"My style is just fine. A fancy waistcoat won't keep me warm on the trails."

Venali stepped closer, reached around Trey for his tea, and brought the cup to his lips, standing firmly inside Trey's personal space. Another inch and there'd be nothing between them. "Keep looking at me as you are, Trey, and we won't make it to AD tonight."

"That's fine with me." Trey set his cup down before he dropped it and lifted his gaze to the male who had tied his heart in knots.

"We'd be missed..." Venali admitted.

Ah, Conor. Of course. Trey wasn't staying, but Conor was, and if Trey kidnapped Venali, Conor would notice. He didn't want to drive a wedge between them, whatever they did or didn't have together. Like Kalie said, it was apparently *complicated*.

"Come," Venali urged, leaving his tea on the side. "If we go early, we can leave early." He was out the room in a few strides, leaving Trey to catch up. They walked the corridors, passing elves who nodded at Venali with respect. Would it be so bad for them to see Venali wasn't immune to hurt? Probably not, but convincing Venali he didn't need to hide was another task entirely. And with Trey not planning on hanging around, he had no right to ask, even if there did seem to be more growing between them than sating lust.

"A few months ago, Alador hinted at some things," Trey began, and then quickly continued before losing his nerve, "and Conor mentioned..." Venali raised an eyebrow. "Look,

73

I'm just going to come right out and ask it. Did you have a crush on me... from the war?"

Venali's mouth twitched. "Kalie said something?"

"And others. My tattoo... You noticed it had changed since I was last here, over a year ago. The only way you'd know that was if you were paying attention."

"Are you suggesting I don't pay attention to prominent assassins who pass through these doors? Assassins who have the ear of Eroan Ilanea no less? Only a fool would ignore you."

Venali had said it all with a straight face and level tone. "So it was just... professional attention?" Alumn, maybe he'd thought too much on it, heard meaning where there wasn't any. "Never mind..." Trey caught Venali's smirk in the corner of his eye. He knew. And he deliberately made Trey squirm on a hook. "Dick."

Venali laughed and opened the door into AD. "I may have had more than a passing interest in you since the war."

Trey arched a brow and sauntered past him. Venali's glare scorched his ass, diverting his attention to the sentinel stalking behind him, so he missed how empty the club was until finding the bar deserted. "Are we early?"

"A little."

Kalie wasn't behind the bar. Nobody seemed to be setting up for the night and the elves who milled around weren't drinking. "Where's Kalie?" Trey asked a female passing by.

"No idea." She shrugged, then eyed Venali like he was next on her to-do list. Venali gave her one of his prized grins but sidled closer to Trey and settled a hand on his arm, seeing off her advances.

"Is she usually late?" Trey asked. He'd have enjoyed Venali's gesture more if Kalie had been here to comment on it.

"Never," Venali said, attention wandering. "AD is her sanctuary. She'll be here."

But as the club filled, others took up Kalie's place at the bar. She clearly wasn't showing. Trey had hoped to say goodbye before he left, but perhaps he'd catch her in the morning. Venali had countless glances and propositions thrown at his feet. He graciously declined them all with a laugh and touch from his smooth gloves.

"You're more of a tart than I was," Trey muttered when the latest interested party slunk off, dejected.

"I've heard about your old ways. Before you became an assassin." Venali leaned closer, bumping his shoulder against Trey's, eyes catching the lamplight. "You had a reputation I've yet to match."

"*Had* a reputation."

"Rumor is you have a lover in every village. You leave a flower on their pillows."

He really had been asking around. Trey hadn't done that in years, but it was true, all of it.

"You've never left me a flower, darling," Venali murmured against Trey's cheek. "After you leave tomorrow, will you go back to those beds?"

Trey tilted his head up, relishing the feel of Venali's smooth chin brushing his cheek. "Would you care?"

"If I said yes," he growled, his fingers claiming Trey's hip, "would you stay longer?"

That seemed like an awfully big question considering they'd only had one drink and the night was still young. Trey rested his head back against the wall, looking up as Venali crowded him close. The sentinel was impossible to see or think around. The things he was asking, it was the lust and wine talking. Venali tipped Trey's chin up. His lips brushed Trey's, stroking a promise across his mouth.

"When you first came to Ashford," he said, slipping his

fingers into Trey's hair and then stroking down his cheek, "everyone watched Eroan. But I watched the marked warrior standing beside him." Venali pressed himself close, leaning his weight inward, his body smothering Trey's in all the right ways. "I only had to look at you to know you cared deeply for Ashford, despite never having been here." Venali's hand found Trey's thigh. His fingers kneaded, approaching Trey's pounding erection only to skip away again. It wasn't enough. Trey sighed out and angled his hips, needing Venali's hand on the hardest part of him. "I know a good soul when I see one," Venali whispered. "And yours is Alumn-bright."

His strong fingers cupped Trey's cock, spilling delicious shivers down his spine. Trey bit into his own lip.

"I saw you in battle," he continued, whispering against Trey's cheek. "In the blood and chaos, I saw you fight dragons. You are righteous and loyal. You are the best of us." His wet tongue flicked over Trey's. "I can't hold your wandering soul for long, but I'll take you while I can."

His words were too great, too heavy, too full of feeling.

Venali's hand squeezed, pulsing pleasure down Trey's arousal, making his head spin and his thoughts scatter.

"Fuck," Trey gasped, "me."

Venali pulled him into motion, through the back door. They made it as far as the corridor outside a familiar room when Venali kissed him hard, his hands tearing at Trey's clothes, trying to dive inside. "I'm going to fuck you so hard —" he moaned into Trey's mouth, "—you'll cry my name as you come."

Trey groaned out something like agreement, too breathless and lost to form proper words.

Venali flung open the door, tripped inside, and froze.

The lamp was lit, the flame spluttering so low it had almost choked itself out.

Kalie lay on the floor, propped against the couch, twin

gashes sliced up her forearms. Her eyes were open. Her mouth too. Like a doll propped there and forgotten.

Shock stole Trey's thoughts. He saw, but couldn't see or think or understand. "Kalie?"

Venali staggered in, dropped to his knees in the shiny pool of blood, and tore off his gloves, reaching for her neck. "I can't... I can't feel. Is she alive?"

Trey jolted forward, shoving the horror aside. He pressed two fingers to her neck, where her pulse should flutter, but felt nothing.

Kalie's eyes stared at the wall. In his mind, he heard her laughing, saw her winking, telling him to fuck Venali already. This wasn't the same Kalie. It couldn't be. He touched her face, smearing blood across her still warm cheek. "Kalie..."

Someone in the corridor screamed.

Venali twitched, looked down at the blood covering his ungloved hand, and scrabbled backward, smearing the glossy dark blood across the floor, coating himself in blood. "Oh, Kalie, no," he moaned, face crumpling.

Another voice behind them. Trey jerked into motion again, falling into the kind of battle instinct that had gotten him through the war. He tore off the floor and blocked the doorway. Already, people were spilling from the club, trying to see what had caused the screaming. "Get Alador," he barked at them. "Go!"

He pulled the door almost closed, but kept an eye on Venali inside, his breaths coming in saw-like gasps. Nobody needed to see Kalie like this, or Venali beside her.

"Is she dead? Is it Kalie?" numerous voices asked.

Rising panic tried to crush his heart. "Just... stay back..."

Alador arrived after what felt like too long guarding the doorway. Someone handed Trey a sheet, and he dutifully covered Kalie's body, only half listening to Alador talk with Venali. The elder's presence lifted a weight off Trey's shoulders and had roused Venali enough for him to explain how they'd found Kalie.

"There's no blade," Trey mumbled, wrapping his arms around himself. He couldn't get warm. He stared at the sheet, watching blood soak through the fabric. "There's no blade," he said again, louder.

Alador and Venali both looked over.

"She didn't do this. Someone took the blade. Someone killed her and left her here." He'd need another look at her, a closer look, to be sure, and really didn't want to peel off the blood-soaked sheet, but he had to know.

Pinching the sheet, he lifted it off again, avoiding Kalie's glassy eyes. Bruises peppered her neck. She'd been held there, choked and attacked.

"Her hands," Venali croaked.

Trey turned her cold hands over. Both palms were shredded. Forearms too. She'd scratched and clawed at her attacker, but it hadn't been enough.

Cold rage numbed Trey's mind. He gently laid the sheet back over her and regarded Alador's stricken face. This was wrong. So wrong.

"Do you need me here?" he asked, sounding cold but not ready to fix that.

Alador blinked. "No, I'll see to it she is properly cared for. You can go."

Trey flung open the door and passed between the guards, avoiding the main club. He made it back to his room before noticing the blood on his hand and clothes. His face, too, he realized, staring at his ghost-like reflection in the mirror.

Assassins weren't supposed to die anymore. He was so sick of wasted lives. So sick of pointless death. "Alumn, why?" It hurt. He clutched at his chest, trying to claw out the pain. Goddess, he couldn't breathe. He hadn't been made for this.

"Trey..." Venali stumbled in through the open door.

"You're leaving?" He was bloody, too, and deathly pale, his fine clothes all disheveled, one glove missing.

"Leaving?" Trey could, he realized. He could walk out, get back on the road. This wasn't his life, his world, not anymore. He'd walked away from Eroan and the assassins for a reason.

"Don't," Venali breathed out, his face stripped of its usual stoic mask. He staggered, movements jerky, as though he didn't know whether to stay or go.

Trey went to him, pulled him close, folded him into his arms, needing to feel him as much as Venali must need this too. Venali slumped against him and shuddered. He folded his hands into fists and crushed Trey to his chest. It was too much. No words could fix this. No drink could chase it away.

"She told me to do something," Venali hissed. "I didn't... and now she's gone."

Trey gripped the sentinel's face with both hands. His eyes shimmered too brightly. Nothing Trey could say would lessen his pain, not yet. Sometimes it felt like no matter what Trey said or did, death still stalked him.

He led Venali by the hand to the bathroom and began to unbutton and unlace his blood-stiffened clothes. Venali did the same with Trey's shirt and trousers, his scarred fingers trembling. The shower washed off the worst of the blood, but Venali still shivered, the chill seeping into his bones.

Trey drew a bath, letting Venali submerge first, to his shoulders. After Trey stepped in, Venali pulled him back against his chest, folding his arm around him, wrapping him close.

Only Venali's soft breathing and the dripping tap upset the quiet. That and the screaming in Trey's head. Trey let his eyes close, unwilling and unable to stop the memories from spilling in. He'd screamed at Nye, yelled at him to stop before his actions got him killed. But it was too late. Nobody knew he'd seen Nye in those last few hours, not even Eroan.

Trey had reached for Nye—his teacher, his lover, his friend—promised him the hurt would end, that he'd take Nye away to heal, but the madness was in his eyes, in his words, and he'd died full of poison and hate. It could have been different. If Nye had just listened, just... taken Trey's hand, Trey could have saved him. Trey saved people, he didn't hurt them. The Order changed that, and war changed everything else.

Venali's hand found his, burned fingers entwining with Trey's.

He rested his head back against Venali's shoulder and let the tears for Kalie, tears for another friend needlessly lost, fall.

VENALI WASN'T in the room when Trey woke. Alone, he lay still, trying to convince himself he'd dreamed Kalie's death. In his mind, he saw himself getting dressed, and tonight, he'd go down to AD and she'd be behind the bar, pouring drinks and flirting.

But someone had ended all that. An Assassin of the Order had killed her; nobody else could get past the door guard into the club.

An Order member had killed their own kin.

Trey closed his eyes.

War changed people, chewed them up and spat them out. And if nobody caught them, they'd fall and keep right on falling.

He couldn't watch another person fall.

He dressed stiffly, hooked his blade into his belt, and pulled his hair back into an Order-style braid. Stern, cold eyes looked back from his reflection in the mirror. He'd thought he'd left that look behind when he turned his back on the killing ways. But nothing of the Order could ever be forgotten. It was all inside, carried with him every day.

He walked Ashford's too-bright-for-winter, sun-soaked, first-floor passageways and entered the atrium from above. Sunlight poured in, setting the tree's colored ribbons ablaze. A female he recognized from AD was climbing the tree, a new ribbon in her hand.

Trey leaned on the rail, a floor above the crowd of grievers gathered below.

Fucking ribbons weren't going to stop this from happening again.

He scanned the crowd. Most all were assassins. The killer was likely among them.

Venali stood beside Alador. The sentinel scanned the crowd, too, perhaps for the killer, or Trey. A male gently making his way toward Venali—Conor. They spoke briefly, and then Conor rested a hand on Venali's shoulder before moving off.

Jealousy spiked. Trey had no right to Venali. He had no plans to stay, and clearly, Venali needed someone who wasn't going to split on him after a few days. The jealousy twisted, turning sour. Trey was the last person Venali needed, but last night, and the bath, and before all that... Venali's honest words about loyalty and light. Trey should have shut it down long before now. He knew better than to make his relationships about more than sex.

He moved on, it was what he did, loving anyone he wanted for a night. Trey was supposed to fall back into that, not get drawn into a life he could never be a part of.

Venali needed Conor or someone like him. An anchor.

Trey left the ceremony.

Returning to his room, he packed his bag. Another night would turn into another and another. But it couldn't last. There was nothing he could do here that Venali already couldn't, just get in his way. It was time to leave. Informing the assistants' desk of his intention to leave before nightfall, he borrowed a pencil and piece of paper from the attendant and took up a spot not far from the tree. Snowflakes fell and melted in the tree's upper branches. Winter waited outside Ashford.

The words for the note came easily. He told Venali he was special, he was loved, that he only had to make it one tomorrow at a time and he'd survive. And it would get easier. Just not with Trey. He signed the note with his name and removed a small wildflower from his pocket. He'd picked it earlier from the gardens after noticing its tiny blue petals poking through the thin layer of snow.

"Trey, I went to your room, but..." Conor noticed the winter boots and coat. "You're leaving?"

Trey stood and handed out the note and flower. "Will you see these get to Venali?"

Conor looked at the note and flower and frowned. "You're just going to go, with everything that's happened?"

Shit, he hadn't expected Conor to care too. "The longer I stay, the harder it will be. Will you... hand this over and just be there for him?"

Conor snatched the note. "Go. I'll give him your fucking note and flower." He whirled and then whirled back again. "It must be nice. To be able to just fuck off when you feel like it." His top lip curled. "Maybe next time you come back around, don't bother finding us." The words rang out through the atrium, reaching more than a few ears.

He could hardly blame Conor for his reaction, but leaving would only get harder the longer Trey stayed. It *was* time to move on. Conor's reaction was proof of that.

Trey collected his messenger backpack and headed out into the snow.

WINTER LASTED LONG into what should have been spring. Trey carried food parcels when he wasn't already laden with trinkets and letters. He wore his feet sore and body lean but delivered every single package, parcel, and note.

Spring finally returned, and along with the bright, chilly mornings and budding flowers, Trey returned to Ashford.

The heavy weight of his backpack said he'd left it too long.

He approached the carved stone archway under blue skies and fresh warmth. Not much had changed. The atrium tree was sprouting new green shoots. Elves and humans still bustled about the many corridors and levels, making Ashford bigger, better, and brighter.

Trey spotted Venali among the guards. His hair had grown long again. Autumnal locks skimmed his shoulders. He looked... leaner. Harder. Or maybe he'd always looked that way? Avoiding the main entrance, Trey took a back pathway into Ashford and delivered his bag without announcing his presence. With any luck, he'd be back on the road in a few days. There was no need to alert Venali or Conor to his presence. Besides, it had been months since he'd left. They'd probably moved on.

He hurried to his allocated room, turning the strange wooden key over in his hand. Only Ashford used keys. There were few locks in the villages he passed through. But Ashford was different. There would be no AD visits this time, no warming another's bed. Strictly in and out.

Rounding the final corner, Trey lifted his head and almost fell over his own feet. Sentinel Venali leaned against the wall outside Trey's allocated room, his arms folded, eyebrow arched.

Trey quickened his pace. There was no reason for this to

be awkward. They were both professionals. He slipped his key into the lock, acutely aware of Venali's simmering a few inches to his left, and opened the door. Two steps inside and the door slammed closed behind him, making him jump and pull to a halt. Venali circled around to face him, like a wolf stalking his prey.

By Alumn, he looked pissed. And he was fucking hot when pissed, his mouth and eyes sharp, his jaw hard and cheek flickering.

"You left," he said.

Trey tasted his pulse. "I have a job to do, the same as you. It was time."

"You left." He stepped closer, close enough that Trey could feel heat crackle off him, or maybe that was Trey's racing heart.

"I left you a note." Alumn, he sounded like a dragon-class dick. Better not to mention the flower too.

Venali's gorgeous eyes narrowed. "I didn't get your fucking note, Trey."

Wait, what? All this time he'd thought Trey had abandoned him? Shit. Trey swallowed hard. "I gave the note to Conor, I—"

Venali clutched the back of Trey's head. His mouth crashed into Trey's with stunning ferocity. The sudden, startling contact flipped common sense and reason on its head. Trey threw an arm around Venali's neck and pulled him in, suddenly, mindlessly, drenched in a torrent of needing Venali plastered against him. He plunged his tongue in, tasting Venali's warmth and spiciness, his tongue sweeping and demanding all at once.

Venali pulled Trey's head back. His mouth scorched a line down Trey's neck.

Trey tore at his sentinel clothes, yanking buckles and ties, growling when they wouldn't easily tear free.

The back of his legs hit the bed. Venali shoved him down.

Venali tore his coat off, freeing the rest of the layers until he stood bare-chested over Trey. Fuck, Trey's mouth watered at the sight of his rippled abs and taut, warm skin.

Venali fell forward, kissing Trey into the mattress, his gloved hands sweeping all over and everywhere. Trey had his hands in Venali's hair, pulling his head to the side hard enough to make the sentinel gasp. Trey licked and bit at his neck, his shoulder, scraping sharp teeth across his skin. More, he wanted more. His hips bucked, body blazing with need. He needed all of Venali now. He'd thought of little else all winter. He needed this troubled, clever, brilliant, beautiful male screaming his fucking name.

Venali kissed him again. His hand dove inside Trey's trousers, grasping roughly. Trey's thoughts tumbled, lost in desperation. Hands roamed and stroked and kneaded. Mouths gasped and groaned and spilled filthy words. Teeth bit and pinched, and by Alumn, Trey was losing his mind. He had no idea where the smooth oil came from but was glad for it when Venali grasped his cock and lowered himself over, sheathing Trey deep inside.

Venali shoved at Trey's chest, forcing him to lay back, and hovered on his knees. Trey's hard cock clenched inside him.

Trey dug his fingers into Venali's naked thighs and arched, seeking more, throwing his head back. Fuck, Venali still looked enraged, even as he rocked, his ocean eyes whipped into a furious storm. Trey held his glare, meeting its challenge, tasting his fury. He dug his nails into Venali, holding him, never wanting to let go again. Venali rode him hard, his mouth flirting with a half snarl, the tip of his tongue skimming his lips. It was more than that. Stripped of the Ashford sentinel uniform, he was exposed and vulnerable, and raw, and free, and everything Trey loved about him.

Venali fell forward. His gloved hand swept up Trey's chest,

his tongue swirled and probed in all the right places, and his mouth claimed Trey's again. How many truly saw him wild, like this? Trey selfishly wanted it to be his secret, his true Venali, and nobody else's. A foolish thought, but one he hadn't been able to shake all through the winter months. He'd hated leaving. Hated himself with every step, knowing it had been wrong, a mistake, but his role as messenger meant he'd been unable to turn back.

He growled, locked Venali against him, and rolled the male over, pinning him to the bed. Venali arched, trying to keep Trey firmly planted inside, but Trey had other ideas. He lifted free, collected the wetness on his fingers, and skimmed Venali's hole, teasing his exposed sentinel, making him growl in frustration.

Alumn, watching Venali gasp, watching his eyes roll and his sharp little teeth bite his lip, Trey wondered how he'd ever walked away from him.

Grasping a pillow, he shoved it under Venali's lower back, propping his hips up, and then the small pot of oil appeared in Venali's gloved palm.

"You came prepared," Trey said, sinking his fingers into the warm oil and plastering Venali's puckered hole, dipping his fingers inside to find that sweet spot and tease it.

Venali threw his head back and sighed hard. "I'm prepared for everything," he said, his voice low and broken. "But not for you. Never for you." He stroked over Trey's hair, the touch so gentle and his eyes so damn soft. Trey's damaged heart cracked some more, letting Venali in. Fuck, this was never meant to mean *more*, but Alumn, it did. It always had.

Trey kissed Venali's mouth, tasting his sweetness and light. He guided his arousal into the sentinel's tight hole, swallowing Venali's rasping breaths with every stroke.

He took Venali's cock in hand between them, wrapping his fingers around the warm, silken shaft, stroked and caressed, listening to Venali pant, feeling his body clench and twitch and shudder.

Venali came, clutching Trey's shoulder, his seed spurting over his flat belly and hip. Trey loosened the hold on his own pace and control, thrusting faster, needing more, needing this glorious male writhing and clutching at him until the lines between them blurred. Ecstasy broke over him, shattering all thought. He came, staring into Venali's gaze, losing his fucking mind and seed as Venali drank him down, body and soul.

THEY TANGLED TOGETHER on the bed, fingers stroking, kisses long and lazy. Trey needed to rediscover every inch of Venali, and more. He didn't know how to say sorry over and over, but he could say it in his touches, say it in gentle kisses. So he lavished Venali in both until they were both spent and buzzed.

"Was there really a note?" Venali lay on his back, Trey pillowed against his chest. His voice rumbled, rough and warm.

Trey pulled back and propped his head on his hand, looking down at his messy, sex-drunk sentinel. "Yes. And a flower."

Venali's auburn eyebrows rose. "You're an asshole."

"If it helps any, I haven't been with anyone else since I left."

The sentinel rolled his eyes. "I have. Many times. Must be every assassin by now."

A curl of laughter slipped free. "Slut."

Venali's chuckles rumbled. "You use the strangest words."

"I pick them up from each village."

Venali shifted onto his side and propped his head up, too,

mirroring Trey's position. "There really wasn't anyone else for you? No quick fuck against a wall, a passing blow?"

Trey shook his head. He'd had plenty of opportunities, and he'd thought about it, but declined every time. There had been only one male on his mind.

"Then it must have been lonely on the road."

Trey rolled onto his back. "I had my hand." He grinned. "A lot."

Venali teased his fingertips up Trey's chest. He'd removed the gloves, making his scarred touch a smooth caress. Knowing he couldn't feel it meant the caress was all for Trey. "No wonder you jumped down my throat," Venali purred, punctuating the sentence by nipping at Trey's mouth.

"That's not what just happened," Trey playfully chided. "You jumped me."

"I'm supposed to be working." His kissing-bites found the corner of Trey's mouth. "Sentinels do not forgo their duties to fuck messengers."

Alumn, it was good to see him smile, to feel him purr and strum and know he was okay. Trey had worried about the sentinel with every step that took him farther away. Leaving had been a mistake, but staying would have been one too.

Venali nuzzled Trey's neck and sighed. "I'm going to be missed..."

You already were. "Did you catch Kalie's killer?" Trey swallowed the knot forming in his throat.

Venali withdrew and sat on the edge of the bed, facing away. "No."

He wished he hadn't asked. "Any more deaths?" He rose onto his knees and swept Venali's hair aside to deliver tiny, tingling swirls of his tongue to the back of Venali's neck. He tasted so good, so warm and soft and spicy. Alumn, he'd missed him, and only now realized how much.

"None."

It should have been good news, but the answers troubled Trey. Four deaths and then nothing? "Stay in bed with me now." He nipped his shoulder.

Venali groaned. "I have to work." Turning his head, he smiled. "Bring your bags to my place. Stay with me while you're here? I'll make us dinner."

"Dinner?"

"Surprised? I have many talents, messenger. If you stuck around, you'd know this."

Trey sheepishly frowned. "I'll be there."

Venali dressed and left after kissing Trey like he was afraid Trey'd leave again.

He was the better male. Trey might not have been so forgiving of his action. Or perhaps Venali didn't care that much to begin with. But he seemed to care, didn't he?

He was too damn good at hiding his feelings. Trey's feelings were all over the place when it came to Venali. He cared for him, more than he should, and it wasn't just the soul-scorching sex. The winter had been the longest of his life for reasons that had nothing to do with the cold and everything to do with walking away from Venali.

Walking away had been easier than staying. Did that make Trey a coward? He had a lot to make up for.

After dressing, he retrieved his bags, and headed for Venali's room on the other side of Ashford.

The main door was unlocked, so Trey went ahead and dumped his bag inside, then took the opportunity to look around. Venali had the kind of subtle eye for beauty in small things. Old, colored glass decorated what would have been stark white walls. He clearly liked light—what elf didn't?—but he'd decorated his rooms in a way that embraced light. The times Trey had visited before, he'd been too distracted to really *look*.

He eyed Venali's bedroom closet and then took a peek

inside. The gorgeous clothes made Trey's traveling outfits look like rags. Each garment was cut and stitched to perfectly fit Venali. Trey salivated at the idea of seeing Venali in every single item and then unwrapping him out of them.

Trey's reflection in a floor-length mirror caught his eye. He wore the same as always, dark-colored trousers, snugly fitted but not too tight, and a sweater that sported a few threadbare patches and holes. Trey looked again at the contents of the closet. Venali wouldn't care if he borrowed something? Just a shirt, maybe a pair of trousers. Venali was slimmer and marginally taller, but the differences were negligible. Trey selected something simple, a boned shirt, clearly designed to emphasize a narrow waist, and black, straight-cut trousers. His reflection told him he cleaned up pretty good. He gathered up his hair, tying it in a loose bun. When he thought of Venali seeing him, flutters shortened his breath. Shit, he was a damned elfling all over again, crushing on the Order assassins because they were the dark and brooding type. It had always been the assassins he'd lusted after, since the second he'd started looking at males differently as a maturing elfling. So proud and strong and heroic. He knew now the truth was far more complicated.

"Venali, about the other day..."

Conor's voice sailed through the main room. Trey winced. Appearing in Venali's clothes was perhaps not the best way to greet the male who'd chewed him out several months ago.

When Trey emerged from Venali's bedroom, Conor was staring at the traveling bag and Trey's blade. He looked up and frowned. "You're back." His mouth formed the strangest wooden smile. "And getting comfortable, I see."

"Venali invited me to stay." Why was this awkward? It never had been before. Trey approached Conor and the male's tension eased some as he took in Trey's attire, apparently liking what he saw.

Trey would welcome that hungry look more once Conor answered a simple question. "Why didn't you give him the note?"

His brow pinched. "The note? Oh, shit, yeah..." He lifted his hands and laughed softly. "I know what you thought you were doing. I get it. You didn't want to hurt him, so you left. That note... Trey," Conor shook his head, "that note would have hurt him. It was better you break away clean, like yanking off a bandage—"

"That wasn't your call to make." Anger frayed Trey's nerves.

"I'm sorry." He shrugged. "I... I didn't think we'd see you again."

And that was the truth. Ditch the note and forget Trey. "I always come back around, Conor."

"Messengers die all the time. You get distracted in other places, with other lovers, maybe you never come around again. We couldn't rely on you. *He* couldn't rely on you. So I did you both a favor."

"Wow." Conor wasn't wrong, but shit, Trey had feelings too.

Conor cleared his throat. "You're right, I guess. I... fucked up." He dropped his head and sighed, and when he next looked up, regret showed on his face. "I had the best intentions. Forgive me?"

He was damned lucky Venali didn't seem to have taken Trey's sudden absence too hard. "Sure." It would take more than saying the words to forgive him, but Trey didn't hold grudges. Life really was too short. "I guess I'm sorry too."

Conor sidled closer and reached toward Trey's face. "Can I make it up to you?"

An uncomfortable sense of wrongness soured Trey's mood further. The three of them had *something*, but it was nothing like Trey felt when alone with Venali. And in truth, he didn't want to share. Not anymore. Trey caught his hand and lowered it between them. "Conor, the times we were together... they were good, but I—"

Conor's hands gripped Trey's hips and yanked Trey hard against him. "You look real good in his clothes."

He lunged for a kiss, the attack so sudden, Trey barely managed to turn his head away. Conor's mouth skimmed his jaw, and then his wet tongue probed at Trey's neck. One of his hands sank to Trey's ass and the other lifted, coming around the back of Trey's neck, pulling him down.

Trey reeled and stumbled against the counter, surprise making him giddy. He didn't want this. He got a hand between them and shoved at Conor's chest, but Conor twisted and plunged in again. His tongue thrust into Trey's mouth, hands suddenly everywhere. Trey didn't remember him being this strong. Trey shoved a second time, tearing his head back.

Conor's fingers wrapped around Trey's wrist and yanked, pulling his arm behind his back. "Dammit, Conor, stop!"

The cool edge of a dragonblade kissed Trey's neck, under his chin.

He froze.

"You never fucking got it, did you?" Conor hissed, pushing on the blade.

Cooling blood trickled down Trey's neck. A twitch and there was no coming back from a blade across the throat. "Stop," Trey hissed. "Remove the blade."

"*You* don't get to tell me when to stop." The blade bit harder. Conor yanked on Trey's shirt, ripping it free of his pants and plunged his hand down Trey's waist, groping inside, his fingernails scratching Trey's stomach. "Neither of you got it! I made it happen. IT WAS ALL ME."

"Con—" The blade cut deeper. Trey closed his eyes and tasted fear's acid bite on his tongue. "Whatever this is, you can talk to me, all right? Just ease off and we'll talk. Nobody needs to know. *I'll help you.*"

Let me help you, Nye. I want to... You don't need to do this...

"Fucking ease off?" Conor thrust his free hand into Trey's hair and pulled, yanking Trey's head to the side. "You don't know what it's like. You can't know. But I'll show you... I'll fucking show you." The words were more animal than elf. "He was mine. He was always mine. And *you* got between us."

Old wounds reopened, old hurts Trey thought he'd buried deep and far where they couldn't ever hurt him again. *I love him, Trey, not you!* Trey heard Nye's voice again, his final words before that toxic love had gotten Nye killed.

Trey gritted his teeth against the rage and fear. History was coming back to haunt him, repeating itself over and over like a curse. Nye had been lost to love, and Conor was too. Trey should have seen it sooner, but he hadn't, because it still hurt. *Everything* hurt. "Get the fuck off me, Conor!"

"It's your fault." Conor yanked him around and shoved him back against the counter. He hissed the next words against Trey's mouth, "*They all died because you got in my way.*"

Oh Alumn, no. Not like this, not Conor. Trey looked into his eyes. Madness looked back. "Please..." Trey whispered, not caring the tears on his face fell for someone else. Someone lost just like Conor was now.

It was happening again.

And Trey's heart couldn't survive it. Not again.

Conor grasped Trey's wet cheeks in his cold fingers and plastered his snarling mouth over Trey's.

It was too much.

Anger thrashed through his veins and snapped free.

Forgetting the blade against his neck, he jerked his knee up into Conor's crotch. The blade pulled across his throat, opening a bloody line, like the lines in Kalie's wrists. The blade... was it the same one used to kill her?

Trey's breath snagged. Conor's hand twisted in his hair and punched Trey down. The counter's edge raced up. Pain exploded through Trey's forehead. And then there was silence.

~

THE BREEZE gently caressing his cheek stirred him awake.

Trey smelled grass and rain and *blood*. Alumn, his face burned. Heat throbbed down the side of his head and across his neck. Breath sizzled in his throat, and when he lifted his head off the ground, groaning out the pain, the noise snagged somewhere behind his tongue, catching on broken pieces.

Something was very wrong with this dream.

Moorland scents were all around him, but he couldn't remember how he'd gotten up here. He tried to get his hands under him to push up but found his wrists were tightly bound in front of him.

Conor.

The blade.

Venali's home.

Blood.

Madness.

His vision blurred. Blinking just made it worse. The fog was worse in his left eye. He could see well enough out of his right eye, and see Conor perched on a rock, the wind lashing his brunette hair about his face.

He looked like Conor but didn't.

The joy Trey had fallen for had snuffed out of his eyes and his bright smile had been torn from his lips, leaving him a colder and harder version of Conor.

Conor picked at the dirt under his nails with a short dragonblade. *Plink-plink.* Blood crusted its edge. Trey's blood. Trey knew that blade, it was the same one he'd found plunged in his door last year inviting him to After Dark. The same blade likely used to rip open Kalie's arms.

Plink-plink.

The world spun, Trey's body loose and distant. He was hurt. Badly. Probably still bleeding. But he was alive. Had the other assassins been given second chances? *Plink.* Somehow, he doubted it.

Alumn, he should have seen the madness in Conor sooner.

Why hadn't he? Had the signs been there? Had Trey *not* wanted to see them?

He needed to think.

He got both his bound hands under him and shoved upright, then wished he hadn't. The world spun some more, trying to take his guts with it. He fell back against a hard boulder.

"Why did you... invite me to AD..." Shit, his voice wasn't working properly. The words scratched, like he'd tried to whisper. "...If you didn't want me there?"

Plink.

Conor frowned at the blade, then stood and sauntered closer. He crouched in front of Trey, looking him over, his face utterly cold.

"*He* wanted you there."

Conor loved Venali. The worse of this was, Trey knew the signs, he'd been in the middle of a broken love before, and he still hadn't seen it when it was right in front of him.

That first night when he'd found the invitation to AD and found Conor at the club, it had all been engineered by Conor. All of it. Even Trey getting him off in full view of Venali. Conor knew Venali had a crush on Trey. Everyone seemed to know it. "You singled me out to get Venali to see you."

Conor's snarl twitched. "Before you... we fucked, but he moved on and I..."

"You couldn't."

"I want him back. You helped and then you left, and that was how it was supposed to be. Just me and Venali. Until you came back."

Fuck, the irony made Trey want to laugh or sob. Nye had been the same, so lost in unrequited love that it had eaten him up inside. Trey had watched him turn from proud assassin into something else, something terrible.

Love didn't have to hurt. Not real love. But it couldn't be forced, either.

Trey must have laughed, because Conor was suddenly on him. The blade's tip tore into Trey's forearm and ripped through his sleeve, tearing downward through flesh.

Trey bucked, tried to tear free, but it happened too fast, and then Conor was backing off, the blade in his hand dripping blood across the ground.

Blood bloomed across Trey's sleeve, ruining Venali's shirt.

It soaked through in seconds and then dribbled from Trey's fingers. Alumn, there was so much of it.

"Fuck..." Trey lifted his bound wrists high, wincing at the throbbing agony. He needed to slow the flow, but he couldn't hold them aloft for long and soon let them fall into his lap.

More blood flowed. It ran in rivulets down his tied, trembling hands and soaked the ground around him.

Kalie had died this same way, her veins torn open, but she'd fought. "You fucking coward..." He wheezed, breathing too hard, body beginning to fail. Panic's claws were sinking in, telling him he was about to die, loosening his tongue and reason. "You butchered your Order kin. Why, Conor?"

Conor shrugged. "It felt good, like nothing else in this world feels good anymore." His grin came alive. "Kalie kept asking about you and Venali. She kept saying how *happy* Venali was. Then she said you were together, and I... made her stop talking. The others were random, just pretty little things with skin that peels open. Making them bleed, watching them die, it gave me a purpose again."

He pressed the blade's tip to Trey's cheek. "Fucking Venali came close—all the power he has, when I'm with him, it's like there's nothing else. I know you felt it too. But it doesn't quite beat sinking a blade into flesh and watching blood trickle away. I started on animals—after the war—watching them die... but it wasn't enough." He flicked the blade, zipping open Trey's cheek, then whirled away, striding a few paces before turning again. "It's power, taking someone's life. You know it. You did it too. We killed dragonkin together, watched them drown in pools of their own blood. *We* did that." He threw his arms up, raising his blade to the sky. "*Alumn, we're Assassins of the Order.* We're kings! We should be worshipped! Instead, we're forgotten, shoved in some basement, pushed aside, told to... I don't know... put down fucking roots and pretend like we're the same as sheep. You can't tame a wolf, tell it to play nice, and then frown at it for killing the weak."

"They weren't weak. They were fucking people! They were Order assassins. They'd earned their right to life... You took that away."

"Oh, don't look at me like that. We all want it. Killing is who we are. It's in our blood. Dragons are gone. We're the predators now."

Trey's teeth chattered. It was cold, wasn't it? The sun was setting, the sky bleeding with him.

Why was he so cold? He didn't feel the wound so much now, or the throbbing in his head. It had all faded beneath the chill in his veins. Trey dropped his head back against the boulder. "Venali knows I'm back. He'll come looking. Let me go now and we can still fix this."

Conor's smile lashed across his lips. "Darling Trey. Venali got a note. You likely remember it? You certainly know how to write a goodbye letter, don't you, Trey. I guess you've had plenty of practice. You should have seen his face fall when he thought you'd left him. Again."

Trey's pulse raced, pumping more blood from the cut. "I don't believe you. I told him about the note. He'll know it's old."

"But your bag was gone, your room empty, and when he asked at the desk, I'd already told them you'd left, so that's exactly what they told Venali. *The messenger has gone*, they said. And it's tragic really, but we'll probably never hear from him again. Messengers die all the time."

"*You son-of-a-dragon's-bitch!*" Trey got his legs under him and lunged, but the moorland tipped and his head spun and Conor slashed with his blade, zipping a line of hurt across Trey's chest. Trey was down again, sprawled among the gorse, breathing too hard. Darkness throbbed in the corner of his vision. A knee plunged into his back, pinning him still.

"When you left last time," Conor hissed, "he almost killed himself, *you selfish prick!*"

The punch landed low on Trey's back, setting off a round of sparks that almost blinded.

"I hate him when he gets like that... Gets stupid, drinking himself into nothing. Venali loves like he lives, hard and fast. He'd have died fast too. I found him out cold on the floor, nearly left him there. But he would have died *for you*, and *you're not fucking worth it.*"

Another punch. Trey's gut heaved. He spat bile and hissed, clinging to the fragments of consciousness, trying to slot them back together. If he passed out, he'd die.

"This is for the best. Your body will be found up here. Wolves will have gotten to you by then. He'll mourn you, but I'll be there for him. *Only me.* None of that bullshit with the three of us."

Venali wouldn't know Conor had killed Kalie and the

others. He'd never know how Trey's life had ended. He couldn't let the truth go unheard. People needed to know. Venali needed to know.

"It... won't work..." Trey rasped.

Conor yanked him off the floor and manhandled him onto his back. "What?"

"You can't... make him... love you."

He snatched Trey's good arm and pressed the blade in. The skin split open, blood pooling. "Say that again—to my face!"

"You're lost."

Conor met Trey's swimming gaze and blinked. The blade stopped its downward cut. Briefly, he almost looked as though he heard the words, like they'd reached into the madness and shone a light onto some small part of goodness inside, and then the smile crawled back onto his lips and the darkness swamped back in.

"Some can be saved... And some can't." Trey thrust his head forward, striking Conor's nose, sending him reeling. He snatched for the blade loose in Conor's hand and pulled it free, only for it to slip from his fingers and tumble to the ground.

Conor plowed into him, tackling him back. Air *oomphed* out of Trey. Conor's fingers clamped around Trey's throat and squeezed.

His weight pushed down.

Trey bucked and shoved, but with his hands bound and his head already half starved of blood, the battle was lost.

His lungs burned, his body twitching out its last desperate thrashes. He let his hands fall.

Conor's grip around his neck tightened. He leaned in, his sneer filling Trey's fading vision.

It would all end here. The truth would never be told. This was what being lost felt like. Like falling, with nobody there to catch you. But Alumn, he had someone. He had a wreck of a sentinel who laughed and loved and fucked up and did it full of passion. It couldn't end here, not now that Trey had finally found a love worth fighting for.

His bound hands rested on the ground. Among the blur of tears, he spotted a rock, its edges jagged. If he could just hold on, and fight, and reach for it...

Alumn, lend me your light.

His fingers found the edges of the rock. It rolled into his palm. *For light, for love, for saving those who want to be saved.* He swung the rock in both hands, smashing it across Conor's cheek.

Conor's grip on Trey's throat vanished. He crumpled to the side, unmoving.

Trey gasped and gulped, then spluttered too much air back up again. It wasn't over. If he had any blood left in his veins, it wouldn't be there long. Rolling Conor off him seemed impossible, but he managed to shove him off enough to pull himself free, and then he was up and staggering. Ashford wasn't far... if he could just...

He fell and choked on sobs. Just a bit farther... Just one more step. Venali needed to know. The assassins needed to know. He got up... somehow... and stumbled on. Cold. Everything was cold and numb now, his body not his own.

"*Who goes there?*"

Relief made his vision swim. His knees struck dirt.

A hand grasped his arm. "Hold on..."

"*Conor*," he wheezed, voice gone, like the rest of him, lost somewhere close to death. But Alumn couldn't have him for her garden, and his ribbon wasn't being tied to the tree. Not today.

~

VENALI SIMMERED in the corner like a flame about to burst and devour all its fuel. He spoke in hushed tones to another assassin, and then he was gone, or Trey had passed out again, because the room was dark. But he wasn't alone. A blade flashed.

He snapped open his eyes and jerked up. The bed, the room, it was unfamiliar. Pain flared across his chest, his neck, everywhere. He croaked out some kind of noise, sounding like someone else.

"Easy."

Venali.

A gloved hand touched Trey's cheek, making him look into Venali's cool green eyes. "Lay back." The sentinel's fragile smile jumped.

"Conor...?" Trey rasped.

"We know. Will you just lay back before you pass out?"

Venali lay him back as Trey tried to keep his eyes open. He needed to know more, but sleep pulled him down again, mixing him into nightmares and dreams full of dead assassins and broken blades.

When Trey woke again, Venali was slumped in the chair beside the bed, head propped on his hand, snoring softly. He'd changed out of his sentinel uniform and wore more casual clothes, still managing to make them look like the height of elegance.

Trey brought his forearms up, wincing at the bandages smothering both arms. It had been too close. He had another bandage he could feel glued to his chest, and one wrapped around the front of his neck. His heart fluttered faster. Too fucking close. He didn't want to die. Planned on never dying, if he could help it, and definitely didn't want to die alone.

Venali's scarred hand covered Trey's, his fingers curling in. It was enough. Any more and the panic clawing up his throat would cripple him more than he already was.

"Shit," he croaked.

"If it's any consolation, your voice is now the hottest thing about you."

Trey looked over and found Venali close, his smile bright and exactly what he needed.

"It was Conor. All of it." Trey cleared his throat or tried to, but apparently the gravelly undertones were staying.

Venali bowed his head. Trey squeezed his hand. Venali probably wouldn't feel it all, but he'd feel something.

"I know. When the guards brought you here, they summoned me. I didn't even fucking know it was you to begin with. The blood... But I saw your arms and how the wounds matched Kalie's."

Trey pulled his hand free and pressed it to Venali's cheek. "He told you I left?"

Venali swallowed. "I believed him."

"He knew what to say to hurt you..."

Venali straightened and then stood and moved to the window. He leaned against the frame, looking out. "It's more than that. I can't..." Tension tightened his shoulders. "We'll talk when you're better."

"No, say it now."

"I can't do this, with you." Venali turned and leaned back against the wall. "The on and off again. Every time you return, I lose my mind over you, and then you leave and it kills me. I can't survive this—us. I'm not..." He flicked his fingers. "I'm not made that way. I either have you or I don't. And if I don't, then fine, but I need to know, because every time I lose you..." He choked off his words and thumped his head back against the wall. "Fuck." His lashes fluttered. "Every time I lose you, I die a little more inside, and there's so little left..."

"I'm sorry—"

"When they brought you in—" Venali struggled with the

words. A grimace pulled his mouth down and his eyes shone too brightly. "I was sure you were dead, and at first, it was... it was another dead assassin, and I knew that was bad. I knew I'd have to go after the killer, but then I saw it was you and I... I froze. Like I froze with Kalie." He thrust his hands into his pockets and looked up. "I froze because I'm in love with you and you were leaving me again and I couldn't stop it from happening."

There were no words, nothing to reply with, no way of fixing this. Alumn, he wanted to. Venali loved him, and suddenly Trey didn't feel worthy of that love. Conor was right, Venali was too bright and fierce and fragile. Trey was afraid he'd break him. Everything he touched seemed to break, especially after the war.

Venali let out an exasperated breath and moved toward the door.

"Wait—"

He turned but looked about the room, staying clear of Trey's face. "Conor is gone... We searched the moor, found where you fought, but he's still out there. I have to stop him." He left, and Trey swore at the empty room. No way was he letting Venali do this alone.

He threw off the blankets, waited for his head to stop spinning, and then gingerly dressed around the bandages. A few healers arrived and tried to fuss over him. He thanked them, ignored their insistence that he stay and rest and heal, and went in search of his blade. Assassins didn't fucking rest *until it was done.*

As VENALI HAD SAID, there was no sign of Conor. Just three-day-old blood. Trey looked at it. He was surrounded by

Ashford sentinels, safe, and well on the way to recovery, but the cold still clung to him.

A week passed, then two. The cuts had all but scabbed over and itched like crazy. They'd leave scars. Now he had some on the outside as well as inside. Conor was likely long gone. He'd have been a fool to stick around. Like Trey was sticking around... delaying his leaving another day, then a week, then more. But Venali had barely said more than a few words in passing.

It *was* time to leave again, and yet... He couldn't walk away again. He was torn two ways, caught between his work and Venali.

Alador had a room alongside all other council members, where he conducted private meetings. Trey lingered outside the closed door. He hadn't knocked, not yet, and probably should, but if he did that, he'd have to speak with the elder, and there was no going back afterward.

"Come in, Trey," Alador's voice rumbled.

The room was small, longer than it was wide, with windows at the back, and a whole load of assassin blades displayed on the walls. Some short, some curved, some fucking mean with fish-hook-like curves. Trey naturally gravitated toward the display. There had to be thirty, maybe more. Each one unique.

"Retired blades," Alador said. He moved from his position seated at the table and joined Trey by the wall. "When they come to me, and they're truly ready to move on, they hand over their blades. I keep the weapons here."

"Why?" Trey's voice still carried a ragged edge that hadn't healed and wasn't likely to. But Venali had said he liked it, which made the change more bearable.

"As a reminder, but also just in case they ever want them back, or they're called on to serve us again, should the dragons return to their old ways."

That was why AD required a blade to enter, because those who went there weren't ready to move on. "I need to explain why I'm not back on the road yet."

"There's no use in leaving too soon. You must heal. Trekking the roads and pathways is not easy."

"No, it's not, but it's not that. Why I've delayed, I mean." Okay, this had been easier in his head. No use in dragging it out. "I'd like to stay in Ashford over winter. I can make myself useful with whatever tasks you have."

Alador's brows lifted. "Just over winter?"

He wanted longer, maybe forever, but he wasn't sure whether Venali would have him, or even if he had any right to ask. "For now."

"Is it to recuperate or... something else? Some*one* else, perhaps?"

"Do I need a reason?"

"No. But I wondered what to tell Venali when he asks why you're still around." Alador smiled.

And of course Alador knew it all. For an ancient elf, he sure kept his ear to the ground.

"He's like a son to me," the elder said, eyeing the blades again. "He feels things deeply, despite presenting exactly the opposite to the sentinels and assassins he guides." He side-eyed Trey. "You pair have a good thing. Don't fuck it up."

Trey blinked and Alador returned to his table, busying himself with rolls of maps. "Ashford owes you a great debt. Of course you can stay. Now, please, go and tell Venali you're staying. Alumn, his brooding is painful to watch."

It felt like the right decision, and with every step toward Venali's room, his heart lifted. He could stay, if Venali wanted him to, and maybe it would become more permanent. Trey wanted it. He wasn't sure if he'd ever wanted anything more.

Venali didn't answer his door. It was too early for AD, but he tried there anyway and found someone stacking the wine and cups, ready for the evening. "I can help," he offered. It would pass the time, waiting for Venali to show.

It wasn't long before Venali did arrive, alone, thankfully. If he'd sauntered in with a string of lovers at the tips of his gloved fingers, it would have made Trey's staying all the more difficult.

"Hello, messenger," Venali purred, eyeing Trey like a cat measuring its prey for lunch. "Filling the time before you leave or are you a server now?"

Trey poured him a drink. "Maybe."

Venali's eyebrow twitched. He lifted the cup to his lips and drank deeply. Trey admired the way his throat moved and imagined mouthing over his fluttering pulse.

"Another, if you please."

Trey poured a second and one for himself, and when Venali lifted his cup, Trey chinked it against his. "I'm staying," he said.

Venali's cup hovered near his lips. "You are?"

"If you want me."

Those piercing eyes narrowed. "For how long?"

Trey shrugged and downed his drink. It scratched down his damaged throat but warmed him through. "However long you want me for."

Venali straightened, his frivolous smile fading. That hadn't been the reaction Trey had hoped for, and as Venali leaned his arm on the bar top and moved closer, Trey's pulse raced. "Don't break my heart, Trey."

Trey leaned in, too, his mouth hovering close to Venali's. "I won't," he whispered, lips brushing Venali's. "I'm staying and I'm yours." Few words had ever felt so right. Trey kissed him painfully softly, the first kiss since he had stumbled half-dead off the moor. A tease and a brush of his lips and tongue. Venali was resistant, guarding his heart. Breaths shared, Trey searched his ocean eyes, falling into their depths. Venali teased a kiss back, his wine-sweet lips delicious against Trey's. And with that kiss, he'd handed Trey his heart.

Venali's hand slipped to the back of Trey's neck. He pulled from the kiss to press his forehead against Trey's. "I love you," he whispered, the crowd and club forgotten. "Your messy hair, your worn-out clothes, your roughness, your nonsense words, and the marks you bear for those you've lost. I love how you see through me. You make me want tomorrow. Please don't leave me again."

"Never." His reply wobbled and not from the damage Conor had done. Trey loved Venali too. He wasn't sure how or when or even why—Venali was a wreck, but he was Trey's wreck. He cared to see him smile, to hear his laugh, to see him happy and safe. Venali deserved to be loved, the good kind of love.

"You need to come home with me right now." He grabbed Trey's hand and pulled him out from behind the bar, then used his body to pin Trey back against it.

"Right now?" Trey teased. Venali smothered him, all sharp angles and lean edges. Venali's eager need prodded Trey's hip.

They made it as far as outside the door to Venali's room before he plastered Trey against the corridor wall and kissed a torturous path down his neck. "I've missed you," Venali panted out. His smooth, gloved fingertips stroked Trey's cheek. "My messy messenger."

Alumn, he felt divine pressed close, like fierce passion bottled in male form. "I'm not going anywhere."

Venali kissed like there was no tomorrow, like this moment was everything in his world, like Trey *was* his world. He didn't deserve Venali's encompassing passion, but he'd try to be worthy, and that had to be enough.

Venali fumbled with the door and shoved it open. They staggered inside, mouths hungry for each other, hands tearing into clothes, seeking hot skin.

A cool, spring-scented breeze pulled Trey's mind away from Venali toward the windows. Broken glass glittered beneath flickering lamplight. The drapes rippled, stirred by the breeze sweeping in through shattered windowpanes.

Venali pulled from Trey's embrace and drifted toward the broken pane. A gust of cold wind blasted in, sweeping his hair back from his face. He turned, his face confused, mouth open to say something—

An arrow streaked across the room, flashing like lightning. It punched into Venali's chest, shoving him sideways, almost off his feet.

Trey sprang forward.

Conor emerged from the bedroom, Venali's bow raised, a second arrow nocked. He drew the string back, making the bow groan.

"No!"

Trey reached for Venali's outstretched hand.

He couldn't stop this, couldn't reach him in time.

The second arrow flew. It slammed into Venali's chest, jerking Venali around. He folded inward, around the pain, staggered, stumbled, and fell against the couch. *No, Alumn, no!*

Trey collapsed to his knees beside Venali and pressed a trembling hand to his chest, skimming around the twin arrow shafts. Warm blood soaked through Venali's shirt. The second arrow had punched in too close to his heart.

Venali breathed too fast; those breaths too short. How many breaths did he have left? Trey touched his face, smearing blood across his pale skin. Venali's eyes said *sorry*.

"Get up!" Conor snapped.

Trey barely heard him. He couldn't look away. Didn't want to hear, to see.

"Get the fuck up or get an arrow in the back!"

"*Get up,*" Venali whispered.

Trey's vision blurred. He couldn't.

Conor pulled on his shoulder. Trey twisted, shaking him off, and stared up the point of an arrow to Conor's hate-filled face.

"You're fucking hard to kill," Conor sneered. "Get up."

Slowly, Trey climbed to his feet. Conor backed off, but the arrow stayed nocked, the string tight. He couldn't hold the weapon armed forever. He would tire. He'd have to lower the bow.

Trey lifted his hands. "Why?"

"You really don't know?"

"I know. I just want to hear you say it." Trey stepped closer, forcing Conor back.

Hate had twisted his face, making him ugly and hollow. The easy smiles and gentle laughs were long gone. Had they ever been real?

"He knew..." Conor jerked his chin. "He knew I killed the others. *You* told him." He grimaced, as though disgusted, but not with his own actions, with Trey's. "He'll never love me now."

Venali's breaths rasped. "It wasn't love."

"You don't know that!" Conor screamed. Tears fell, wetting his face. He relaxed the bow's string and lowered the bow, but still held the arrow nocked. "You don't know because you hardly even saw me! I loved you and you threw me away like I was just some cock to pass the time!"

"You were."

Conor swung the bow toward Trey.

"Don't!" Venali cried out.

"Watch each other die!" Conor's fingers slipped from the string, setting the arrow free.

Trey jerked aside. The arrow sailed past. He dashed forward and slammed the ball of his hand under Conor's jaw, slamming Conor's head back, rocking him on his feet. Trey landed a punch in his gut. Conor buckled. He should have reeled, should have fallen, but he threw his arms around Trey's waist and tackled him with a roar. Trey's back hit the windows. Glass cracked. Conor slammed his forehead into Trey's. Trey's head smacked back, his vision splintering. So fast, too much. Glass cracked again. If the window failed, they'd both fall through. *Just die!*

An arrowhead burst through Conor's throat.

Everything stopped.

Conor's eyes flew wide. He shook his head, mouth opening and closing, and stumbled backward. Venali wavered on his feet, stepping aside. He let Conor drop to his knees, skin turning blue, his eyes blurring with blood. He slumped over and collapsed facedown.

Venali staggered.

Trey rushed in, catching him as he crumpled. He clung to Trey, half smiling. "I think I need your help."

"I've got you." Trey scooped him up, careful to leave the arrows in situ, and carried him to the door.

"I know you do," he whispered, head resting on Trey's shoulder. His eyes fluttered closed.

"Alumn can't have you," Trey choked..

Don't take him, Alumn.

Please don't.

Not him.

I need him.

I love him.

Venali mumbled, "I'm yours." He fell limp in Trey's arms, soft breath sighing out. If those were his last words, Trey wouldn't survive them.

Trey hugged him close and ran from the room.

THEY TIED another ribbon to the tree. Trey watched it flutter with the others. So many dead. So many loves lost. After everything they'd fought for, after living lives devoted to saving others and fighting impossible monsters, it didn't seem right that any assassin should die.

Trey closed his eyes and bowed his head.

A gloved hand slipped into his and squeezed. A warm, little smile lifted Trey's lips. Venali's shoulder bumped his, making him look. Sunlight caught in Venali's hair and touched his cheeks, warming his rare freckles. With his face lifted to admire the tree, light played across its perfection.

To think he'd almost lost him cinched Trey's heart and shortened his breaths.

"He never was very good with a bow," Venali whispered, his smile twitching.

The second arrow had missed Venali's heart by less than an inch. Conor's aim had been true. Maybe some part of Conor steered the arrow off course, or maybe he was just a poor shot.

After two weeks in recovery, Venali had escaped the healers and tried to convince Alador he was fit for sentinel duty. But the scar over his heart went deeper than the mark on his skin. It would take more than a few weeks to heal the inside.

Alador moved through the crowd toward them now. "You wanted to speak with me?"

"I do, yes," Trey replied. Venali gave his hand a squeeze again and let him go, so he could draw Alador to one side, away from the ceremony.

"How is he?" Alador asked, nodding toward Venali standing beneath the tree.

"Better, I think. You know how he is."

"I do." Alador's smile was a warm one, leaving Trey with no doubt that Alador deeply cared for Venali.

Trey unclipped his dragonblade and offered it up with

both hands. The blade meant everything to him, but it was also from a part of his life he was ready to let go. "Will you keep it safe for me?"

Alador looked at the blade and sighed. "I'll have to write to Eroan and explain."

"I have a feeling he'll understand."

Venali's attention warmed Trey's back. Trey hadn't told him he was officially retiring, but he'd known, like he seemed to know all the important things without having to ask.

Alador took the blade and bowed his head. "Thank you, Trey. For your service and your kind heart. Your impact here has not gone unnoticed. We're honored to have you settle among us."

"I'm honored to be here," he glanced toward Venali, saw him looking over, and added, "and to be with him."

Alador's warm, steady hand landed on Trey's shoulder. "I suppose I need to find a new messenger. Though, you're irreplaceable."

"I like to think so," Trey grinned.

"Perhaps you can convince Venali to hand over his bow?" Alador nodded toward Venali, prompting him to start heading over.

Venali wasn't ready. "One day, maybe." When he was as old and wizened as Alador.

Venali dipped his chin in respect and noticed Trey's blade in Alador's hand. He lifted his sizzling gaze to Trey.

Alador smiled. "It takes someone very special to settle a wandering soul. May Alumn's light guide you both." He nodded and left to mingle among those at the ceremony.

Venali moved in closer, placing a gentle touch on Trey's hip. Gentle or not, it still sizzled with the promise of where that touch might go next. Trey wet his lips. He'd never get enough of Venali.

"You hung up your blade..." he purred, sidling in close,

"Does that mean you're all mine? No more flowers on the pillows of strangers?"

Trey rested both arms over Venali's shoulders and drew him close enough to kiss, nudging his mouth, then pulling back to bump his forehead against Venali's. "I've been lost for as long as I can remember." Wandering from place to place, his heart seeking something he wasn't sure existed. He'd thought he'd almost loved with Nye, but when that all broke apart, it had broken Trey apart too. Until now.

"I know how that feels," Venali whispered.

And now there was Venali, picking up the pieces of his heart and slotting them neatly back together with precise, careful fingers.

"Somehow, I found you, with your harem of lovers, your ridiculously stunning clothes, your ruthless pursuit of pleasure, and your prickly exterior hiding a vulnerable heart. And I love you for all those things."

Venali's lips curved into a genuine smile. "You found the real me." He moved in, his mouth brushing Trey's.

"We'll have to talk about those lovers."

"Hm," Venali purred, hands clasped on Trey's hips, gently rocking. "There are no other lovers and haven't been for a long time. You carry my heart, messenger. Promise me you'll keep it safe."

Trey kissed him soft and slow and full of care, knowing the impossible male in his hands was as fragile as he was strong. This was his life now, and he couldn't wait to live the tomorrow alongside Venali.

The End

SILK & STEEL (EXCERPT)

roan

THE IRON DOOR rattled on its hinges and groaned open, spilling silvery light inside. Gloom fled to the corners, leaving behind a figure with broad shoulders. *Male*, Eroan thought. Curious scents of warm leather and citrus tickled his nose. After the wet and rotted smell of the prison, he welcomed any change in the air, even if it meant his visitor had returned.

Eroan kept his head low and his eyes down, hiding any signs of relief on his face. The shackles holding his wrists high bit deeper. He'd been so long in the dark, he'd almost forgotten he was a living thing. The constant, beating pain was a cruel reminder. This visitor was a cruel reminder too.

He knew what happened next. It had been the same for hours now. Days, even.

The male came forward, blocking more light, lessening its stab against Eroan's light-sensitive eyes. He turned his face away, but the male's proud outline still burned in his mind. Other images burned there too. The male's half-smile, the glitter of dragon-sight in his green eyes. Eroan had rarely gotten so close to their kind without killing them.

His mission would have been successful if not for this one.

"You need to eat." The male's gravelly undertone rumbled.

He needed nothing from *him*.

A tray clattered against the stone floor. The sweet smell of fruit turned Eroan's hollow stomach.

Moments passed. The male's rhythmic breathing, slow and steady, accompanied the scent of warm leather rising from his hooded cloak, and with it the lemony bite of all dragonkin. A scent most elves were taught to flee from.

"Were you alone, elf?" the dragonkin asked. The questions were the same every time. "Will there be another attempt on her life? How many of your kind are left in our lands?" More questions.

Always the same. And not once had Eroan answered.

Steely fingers suddenly dug into Eroan's chin, forcing him to look, to *see*. Up close, the dragonkin's green eyes seemed as brittle and sharp as glass, like a glance could cut. His smile was a sharp thing too.

"I could torture you." The dragonkin's smile vanished behind a sneer.

Eroan's straining arms twitched, and the chains slung above his head rattled against stone. *He has me in body*, *but not in spirit.* He gave him nothing, no sneer, no wince, just peered deep into the dragonkin's eyes. Eyes that had undoubtedly seen the death of a thousand elves, that had witnessed villages burn. If they had souls, this dragon's would be dark. *He could torture me. He should. Why does he wait?*

Eroan recalled that cold look when their swords had clashed. He'd cut through countless tower guards, severing them from their life-strings as easily as snipping at thread, but not this one. This one had refused to fall. This dragonkin had fought with a passion not found in the others, as though their battle were a personal one. Either he truly loved the queen he protected, or he was a creature full of fiery hate that scorched whatever he touched.

The dragonkin's fingers tightened, digging in, hurting, but just as the pain became too sharp, he tore his hand free and stepped back, grunting dismissively.

Eroan collapsed against the wall, letting the chains hold him. Cold stone burned into raw skin. His shoulder muscles strained and twitched. Pain throbbed down his neck too, but he kept his head up, kept it turned away.

"I cannot..." Whatever the dragon had been about to say, he let it trail off and reached for the ornate brooch fixing the cloak around his neck, teasing his fingers over the serpent design.

Eroan wondered idly if he could kill him with that brooch pin. Of course, to do that, he'd need to be free.

The dragon saw him watching and dropped his hand. "You do not have long, elf." His jeweled eyes glowed. Myths told of how the dragonkin were made of glass and forged inside great fire-spewing mountains in a frozen land. Not this one. This one had something else inside. Some other wildfire fueling him.

The dragon turned, sweeping his cloak around him, and headed out the door.

"What is your name?" The question growled over Eroan's tongue and scratched over cracked lips. He almost didn't recognize the rumbling voice as his own.

The dragon hesitated, then partially turned his head to peer over his shoulder. The fire was gone from his eyes, and something else lurked there now, some softer weakness that belied everything Eroan had seen. His cheek fluttered, an inner war raging.

The answer would have a cost, Eroan realized. He shouldn't have asked. He let his head drop, tired of holding it up, of holding himself up. Tiredness ate at his body and bones. The shivers started up again, rattling the chains and weakening his defiance. This dragonkin was right. He did not have long.

"My name is Lysander."

The door slammed, the lock clunked, and Eroan was plunged into darkness.

~

THE DRAGON QUEEN'S reign is one of darkness and death. Humans have vanished under the rubble of their world and if the queen has her way, elves will be next.

EROAN, one of the last elven assassins, lives for one purpose: kill the queen. He would have succeeded if not for her last line of defense: Prince Lysander. Now, captured and forced into the queen's harem, Eroan sees another opportunity. Why kill just the queen when he can kill them all? It would be simple, if not for the troubled and alluring prince. A warrior, a killer, and something else... something Eroan finds himself inexplicably drawn to.

TRAPPED IN A LIFE HE DESPISES, Lysander knows his time is running out. If the queen doesn't kill him for his failures, her enemies will. There's nothing left to live for, until an elf assassin almost kills him. A stubborn, prideful, fool of an elf who doesn't know when to quit. An elf who sparks a violent, forbidden desire in Lysander. If Lysander can't save himself, maybe he can save the elf and maybe, just maybe... one stubborn elf will be enough to bring down the queen before she kills them all.

DUTY DEMANDS they fight for their people. Love has other plans.

ALSO BY ARIANA NASH

Writing dark fantasy LGBT

Sealed with a Kiss, 0.5 Silk & Steel

(free to Ariana Nash newsletter subscribers. Sign up at www.ArianaNashBooks.com)

Silk & Steel, Silk & Steel #1

Iron & Fire, Silk & Steel #2

Blood & Ice, Silk & Steel, #3

The Black Prince (Akiem's story)

And coming next year: dark battle angels in, *Primal Sin*. Visit Ariana Nash's reading group on Facebook for all the news as it happens.

ABOUT THE AUTHOR

Born to wolves, Ariana Nash only ventures from the Cornish moors when the moon is fat and the night alive with myths and legends. She captures those myths in glass jars and returning home, weaves them into stories filled with forbidden desires, fantasy realms, and wicked delights.

Sign up to her newsletter here: https://www.subscribepage.com/silk-steel

Made in the USA
Las Vegas, NV
05 April 2025